Once Upon a Book

A Create-Your-Own-Quest Novel

Faith Colleen Weaver

To Jonelle
You always have a choice!

ELK LAKE PUBLISHING INC
PUBLISHING THE POSITIVE
Plymouth, Massachusetts

Cover and Interior Design: Derinda Babcock

Illustrations: Holly Rogers

Editor(s): Sue Fairchild, Deb Haggerty

PUBLISHED BY: Elk Lake Publishing, Inc., 35 Dogwood Drive, Plymouth, MA 02360, 2020

Library Cataloging Data

Names: Weaver, Faith Colleen (Faith Colleen Weaver)

Once Upon a Book—A Create-Your-Own-Quest Novel / Faith Colleen Weaver

242 p. 23cm × 15cm (9in × 6 in.)

Identifiers: ISBN-13: 978-1-64949-024-7 (paperback) | 978-1-64949-025-4 (trade paperback) | 978-1-64949-026-1 (e-book)

Key Words: Action/Adventure, Fantasy, Young Adult, Interactive, Literature, Challenges, Trust
LCCN: 2020950869 Fiction

DEDICATED TO:

My mama. Thank you for always believing in me and never letting me settle for mediocre. (Even if I didn't like you too much throughout the editing process.) Thank you for teaching me to never stop dreaming. I love you.

DISCLAIMER:

Neither Elk Lake Publishing, Inc. nor I, Faith Colleen Weaver, support the racial prejudice depicted in the classic novels or by their authors. However, in an attempt to not erase history, I have chosen to quote these classics in their original forms because to do otherwise would to be to pretend the bias never existed.

ACKNOWLEDGMENTS

WOW! This has been quite the adventure. And no adventure should be taken alone. So, I'd like to take the space to thank those who joined me for this incredible journey:

My husband, John, for standing by my crazy idea and being my biggest support.

My mama, for being my editor in chief and biggest fan.

My sister, Holly, for creating the amazing illustrations.

Katelyn, for pushing me to reach my potential when I wanted to give up.

Deb Haggerty, for taking a leap of "Faith" on me and my ideas.

Sue Fairchild, for being a phenomenal editor and cheerleader.

Marsha Hubler and the Montrose Christian Writers Conference. Without you all, I wouldn't be a writer to begin with.

And finally, my friends and family for always supporting my dreams.

Oh, and my cats, for their moral support.

THE BEGINNING

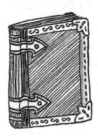

The ivy-laced, stone towers connecting the walls surrounding Ashkelan loomed like protective guards on every side. Each bend in the fifty-foot barrier kept me from the outside world. Not that there was much out there to see since the entire population lived within the walls.

A common game among the young ones of the city consisted of trying to sneak, unnoticed, into one of the forbidden towers. The game became more of a dare as children began disappearing once inside. At seventeen, I'd had my fill of the classic run around the tower perimeter and sought to travel farther into the depths of this hidden treasure. Most of the older kids explored a different room each time they entered the beast of a turret. Each came out with a story to tell of adventures within. Some never returned at all. Today was my turn.

After sneaking through the main corridor of the tower, I found myself in a place where I knew I didn't belong. I surveyed the low-lit room, which certainly didn't look dangerous or capable of destruction and chaos. I jerked my gaze to the countless shelves surrounding me, each carrying thousands of mysterious books. I pulled a book from one shelf and opened it. I stared at the scattered letters scrawled before me, each combination swirling into a word, drawing me further into the pages, captivating my mind and entrancing me. The Answers told me from the time I could speak that reading was a dangerous practice and forbidden to all those living within the walls of Ashkelan. But how could they expect me to stay away from such a wondrous thing once discovered? The pages, light in weight, held something much more substantial. The outer core smooth, edged with a spine containing an entire lifetime living within. The heaviness of the item rested easily in my hands as if I could bear a thousand of these small worlds. Even the smell intoxicated me—a sense so familiar and relaxing that contrasted with the anxiety rising within me. I shouldn't have been there, but now, how could I leave?

A voice told me to open each one and read every word available to me. But wait ... what voice? I was alone. I heard the words resonate in my mind. *Maybe the Answers are wrong.*

The book fell from my hands and hit the cold stone floor with a thud. The noise sounded deafening against the silence of the room, and I knew I didn't have much time. I swallowed a scream and ran.

Bursting through the doors of the library, I almost knocked into a huge marble pillar along the wall. Gathering my wits, I ducked behind it, trying to stay concealed in the shadows. Never in a million years had I expected to hear a voice in my head, something only spoken of in legends. The Answers told of dangerous ones who had voices in their minds controlling them. Trained to fear those who had this internal voice, I had prayed to never hear one. Now here I was listening to the very thing I was taught to dread.

★★★

If you want to know the BACKSTORY *turn to page 3*.
If you want to know WHAT HAPPENS NEXT *turn to page 5*.

BACKSTORY

Once upon a time, the world was "normal." Reading and learning were natural occurrences, and books were being written everywhere. Those who read became strong and wise, though they rarely realized their powers. A singular group, who did not intend to start the world on its downward spiral, noticed changes in those who read. This class of scientists started studying the readers of the time and observed them growing stronger and more powerful with every word.

The scientists feared those with the power and began putting them through mental tests in an attempt to control their abilities. The tests, however, did not go as planned once the subjects realized their full potential and started acting out. Locking the readers away, the scientists destroyed their minds with torturous games and tricks to convince them the world would be better off without their precious books.

Many authors and readers went into hiding as this crazed group of scientists and their brainwashed minions started a hunt to find and conscript all book lovers into their society. The group called themselves the "Answers," believing they knew what was best for all humankind. Those in hiding began writing in secret, attempting to leave clues and codes behind, hoping someday a reader would find them and unlock the answer to free the land of the horrific trail it seemed to be traveling.

ONCE UPON A BOOK

Now, hundreds of years later, the Answers still ruled the land, conscripting new members every year and becoming more powerful day by day. They created a walled city called Ashkelan and locked the entire population inside. Guards patrolled not only the perimeter, but also the one location where books still lived, a hidden library. The Answers didn't know about the group still in hiding, however, and all that group needed was a single answer.

***

Continue to WHAT HAPPENS NEXT *on page 5*.

WHAT HAPPENS NEXT

Calm down. Be quiet! The jarring sound coming from within me made being quiet nearly impossible as my ragged breathing and heart rate increased to a roar. *Be invisible. Wait! Footsteps? What if you get caught?*

I willed the voice to be quieter than my breathing as I stared down the grand hallway, praying there were no guards on their way toward my hiding spot.

"Speak and you'll never breathe again."

A small gasp escaped my lips as a rough hand pushed the sound back into my lungs before it could escape and pulled me deeper into the shadows. A cloak surrounded my petite form and a rough panel scraped across my back as the wall opened to reveal a small crevice. Once inside the dark corridor, my captor released his grip and lit a minute torch seemingly out of nowhere. His eyes flashed an almost electric blue in the firelight.

I backed against the hard stone. "Do I know you?" My thin wisp of voice barely escaped my mouth before dissipating into the air.

"I'm not going to kill you if that's what you're worried about. Follow me or be lost, your choice."

He didn't glance back as he strode down the hall like he owned the place. I peeled my body away from the damp wall and crept along behind the mysterious stranger.

Each step echoed as I fought the voices yet again. *He's familiar ... that dark hair, the blue eyes ... I know him from somewhere.*

An eternity passed as the silence around me collided with the rampant screams inside my mind. The voices grew louder, blurring my vision and making breathing difficult. I stopped and gasped for the air these voices had stolen. I collapsed to the floor of the tunnel, shaking with every staggered breath.

My captor's boots entered my vision as his voice broke through the cavalcade of torture inside me.

"Don't worry, they will pass with time. The dizzy spells, I mean. They go away once you get used to the voices."

I stared up at him. "How did you know about the voices?"

"Because I have them too." With that, he turned and continued down the passage, leaving me to struggle to my feet and stumble to catch up.

After another silence, he stopped. "You know you're in danger, right?"

His sudden concern caught me off guard. "Why? Because I have voices in my head?" Saying the words aloud made them almost seem real.

"Yes, exactly. The Answers, they ... they destroy minds like ours." He looked away, but not before I caught a flicker of emotion flash through his icy eyes.

"Hey, are you all right?" I stepped toward him, but he backed away.

"Don't come near me. I'm still infected."

Another emotion ... shame.

"Infected? What are you talking about?"

His gaze met mine. "If I answer that, will you answer a question for me?" I found keeping track of this guy's emotions difficult. Now, his eyes pleaded like a child.

I nodded.

"When the Answers induct a new member, they brainwash them, causing them to forget anything except what the Answers tell them." He paused. "I was inducted almost ten years ago. But somehow, I managed to keep some of my own thoughts. That's what those voices in your head are by the way, your own individual thoughts. I've been fighting the machines they put me in, exercising my thoughts, and exploring the grounds. I found these passageways months ago, and today, I decided to escape for good."

"So, you're a fugitive from the Answers?" My heartrate quickened.

"All of my explanation, and all you got was that I'm a deserter?" The man almost smirked but returned to an emotionless stare.

"That's terrible." I hesitated. "But why would they want to brainwash you? How do they choose who to take?"

"They only take people who can read."

My heart seemed to stop completely this time. "I ... I can read," I whispered.

"I know. That's why I saved you. I need your help. But first, you promised to answer my question."

"Oh, yes ... I did. What is it?"

"Do ... do you know who I am?" His gaze dropped to the floor. "I kept a few of my thoughts, but they managed to erase my memories. I have no idea who I am."

"I'm sorry I ... wait ..." I did a double take at the memory I saw but those eyes were undeniable. "Axen? Is your name Axen?"

The man's eyes blitzed another shockwave as his body twitched at the name. "Yes, it is. I ... I remember!" He beamed at the realization. "Did you know me?" His eager voice made his intimidating demeanor vanish.

"Not really, but I knew of you. I saw you the day you entered the tower. I was only ten at the time."

Axen soaked up the information and leaned back against the wall of the tunnel. "Is that all you remember?"

"So much has happened, I'm not even sure what I know and what I don't. I'm sorry."

"It's okay. You've already given me my name, and that's a start. Thank you." He paused. "Wait, I never asked your name."

"Calessa."

"Well, Calessa, I may not remember my past, but I know a lot about our future. There are more readers outside the city, and we need to get to them and fast. How are you at climbing?" Axen motioned to a trapdoor in the wall at least twenty feet above our heads.

"Umm, not that great."

Axen grunted and turned to face another tunnel leading to pitch black. "Well, the wall meets the ocean down that way. How about swimming?" He turned back to me with raised eyebrows.

I looked up at the trapdoor and then down the gloomy, damp passageway. I never expected to leave Ashkelan, let alone escape with a fugitive. *Maybe following him wasn't such a good idea.* I shut my eyes and willed the voice silent. This was going to be an adventure.

***

To escape OVER THE WALL, *turn to page 9.*
To escape UNDER THE WALL, *turn to page 15.*

OVER THE WALL

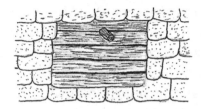

"My swimming skills are basically nonexistent."

Axen tugged at a loose rock on the wall. "All right, up and over it is. I hid some supplies the last time I was exploring." The rock gave way and revealed a small cavern in the base of the wall. Axen pulled a crate from inside and began emptying the contents onto the muddy floor.

I looked at the scraggly rope and moldy papers laying before me. "How are these supplies?"

"You'll see, but we have to move quickly. They are going to be right on our tail the moment they realize I've breached the wall."

Axen circled one end of the rope and then secured the noose with a tight knot. Tossing the looped side toward the trapdoor, he managed to catch the small rock acting as a knob and pulled the door open. The loud grinding of the door against the rocks made my insides shiver. Axen unhooked the rope and threw it once again at the trapdoor opening, this time catching hold of a rock next to the opening. Giving it a slight tug to test its hold, Axen then let the rope fall limp against the wall.

"It's only going to hold one of us at a time. Wait here." Tucking the papers into his leather jacket, Axen approached the rope. He scaled the wall like doing so was the simplest feat. Within seconds, he'd disappeared into the trapdoored hole and was now peering down at me.

"Come on, let's go."

I nodded, my hands shaking as I walked toward the rope. *What are you doing? Get out of here. Now's your chance.* The voices rambled on, convincing me not to follow Axen. *You don't know him. He could get you killed. He's a fugitive. You don't want to be in this mess. Run! Now! Before it's too …*

The voices died out as I looked up to see those startling blue eyes staring down at me. Grabbing the coarse rope in my hands, I began to climb.

My ascent was not nearly as graceful as Axen's, but I managed to reach the top with minimal rope burn and only two small cuts on my arm from where the jagged cave walls had gotten the better of me. When I was close enough, Axen extended his hand and pulled me into the opening. I stood on shaky legs and surveyed our new locale. The small cavern had no obvious exits and seemed to be solid rock at every turn. *Great! Now we're stuck up here.*

Turning to Axen to convey my thoughts, I heard noise from the tunnels below. Axen must have heard it too because he dove to the opening and frantically pulled the rope into our hiding spot, shutting the trapdoor as the shouts and footsteps from below echoed in the cavern where we had stood just moments ago.

"Now what?" Keeping my voice low, I motioned to the relentless walls surrounding us.

Axen silenced me with a look and pointed to a side of the cavern with grooves every few feet leading up to another small door in the ceiling. Motioning me to stay close, he began climbing the makeshift ladder. When he'd reached the ceiling, he pushed the door to reveal a sliver of sunlight, shattering the darkness my eyes had adjusted to. Shielding my eyes with my hand, I blindly followed Axen into the brightness, and we scrambled out onto the hot stones of the outer wall. As my eyesight adapted to the light, I stood to dust off my filth-covered pants only to come face to face with a view I had only heard about.

"Wow."

The world stretched much farther than I could ever have dreamed. Brilliant blue water splashed against the side of the walls and a sparkling clean beach extended on for miles. High cliffs surrounded the shoreline and acted as a barrier between the white sands and the green forest covering the rest of what I could see. My breath caught in my throat as I realized how much lay beyond our city walls.

Axen was suddenly next to me. "Calessa, are you all right?"

"I never knew …" I paused and looked around me. "I never knew any of this existed. I always thought the outside world was bare and dark. I never would have dreamed it was so beautiful."

"If everyone knew what the outside was like, it would be much harder for the Answers to keep everyone in." Axen started down a small set of stairs scaling the outer side of the wall. "Come on, we don't have much time left."

I followed reluctantly, not wanting to lose the amazing view. The stairs were narrow and steep, a treacherous descent. I clung close to the wall but kept my eyes on the spacious landscape that grew bigger with each step. I tripped as my boot landed in the sand. I had never walked on something so soft. Before I could adjust my footing, I heard a new voice—and not inside my head this time.

"Stop! Fugitives from the law will be put to death!" I looked up to see two guards atop the wall. Axen grabbed my arm and pulled me along as he broke into a run across the sand. We raced down the beach, the guards scrambling down the staircase in pursuit.

Rounding a bend, Axen slid into a crevice in the rocky siding of the cliffs lining the beach. I slipped in after him and waited for the guards to pass. Axen's rough hand slid into mine and pulled me further into the darkness. The small tunnel widened, and I struggled to see where we were going. Despite the dimness of the passageway, I could see a warm glow of light ahead as we walked deeper into the cliff. The spark of light came from a single lantern hanging in the tunnel.

"Where are we?" I whispered.

"We're at the entrance of the hideout. Like I said, there are readers here in the outside world who have hidden from the Answers. This is where we'll find them."

We followed the path for a while, only to come to a dead end. A single lantern dangled from the low ceiling. My mind whirled again. *This was a mistake. You must be crazy to think you can outrun the Answers.* Before I could ask what we were going to do, Axen reached out and felt along the wall.

"There's a door here. I just have to figure out how to open it." He grabbed the lantern off its hook and stepped closer to a smooth section of the cavern wall. "There's something written here. 'Two hands over and one hand down, there the secret door is found.'"

Axen moved his hand to the side of the script and then down. Pressing against the wall, a loud grinding noise erupted from behind me. I turned as a slab of rock disappeared into the cliff wall and revealed the second most extraordinary sight I had ever seen.

Splayed out before me was a small underground city made of wood and stone. Gardens surrounded many of the homes and a creek flowed across the scape with a rickety bridge connecting the town to the mossing land. As the door opened, a few people milling about turned to see who was invading their secret world. I stepped through the opening, and then looked up to see hundreds of lanterns hung from the great expanse above.

An old man hobbled across the bridge toward us. "Welcome strangers. Who are you?"

"I'm Axen and this is Calessa. How do you know we aren't a threat?" Axen stepped up to the man as he spoke.

"Only those who read can find the door. You are here, therefore you can be trusted." The old man chuckled. "I am

Aldred. The keeper of this city. Are you from one of the other tribes?"

I looked at Axen. "Other tribes?" Axen's response proved he didn't have much more information than I did. "I thought this was the only hideout?"

"Oh, no." Aldred shook his head. "This is but only the first of the many refuges built in the last one hundred years. If you are not from the other tribes, you must be from Ashkelan."

This question I knew the answer to. "We are," I said. "Axen is a fugitive and I am ... well, I suppose I am too."

"You will be safe here. If you are willing, however, we could use your help. Do you know anything about the Final Answer?" Aldred's eyebrows rose and his eyes sparkled.

Axen responded instantly. "It is the one answer that will free all of us who were brainwashed. If spoken at the heart of Ashkelan, the torment will be over, and we will be able to think and read as we once did."

Aldred smiled and nodded. "I see you have been conscripted. You are lucky you escaped when you did. What about you, dear?"

"N-no. I didn't even know I could read before today."

"I see." Aldred motioned behind him to the small group of people gathered to gawk at the newcomers. "As you can see, we here at the original base are getting older and cannot go out as we used to. We need someone to travel to the other camps and see if they have found anything to move us closer to the Final Answer we seek. I am a young one-hundred and four years old, but even I won't live forever. I just hope to see the world returned to its original state before I go." He looked at us with a critical if not saddened gaze. "Will you help us?"

"I will." Axen spoke with authority before turning to me. "Calessa, you are free to stay here where it is safe."

The voices in my head started arguing. *Don't go. Stay where it's safe. No, go. Follow your heart and help these people. But I could be killed. But I could save the city!* I stared at Axen for a moment and his look gave me courage. "No, I will go with you. We'll be safer together."

"Thank you." Aldred sighed and turned to his village. "You can stay here tonight and get a fresh start in the morning. We have a map to guide you to the next camp. There have been rumors they have the first key to the Final Answer."

Aldred led us to a small home near the edge of the town. Inside, a shelf with a few tattered books caught my eye. Aldred went to them and pulled a ragged piece of paper from between some of the pages.

"There are two ways to reach the first camp." He spread the paper out on a table and gestured for us to join him. On the worn sheet was a map, showing two routes ending in the same place. "You can either go up a tunnel that leads into the densest part of the forest or you can climb the cliffs and make your way around the outer edge of the woods. Either way, it will take you about a half day's journey. It's your choice, though both come with challenges. Once there, tell them you came from the base camp. They will know my name. But decide that in the morning. For now, let's get you two something to eat and some fresh clothes."

The rest of the evening passed in a blur as we were introduced to the rest of the villagers, given food, and set up on two cots for the night. The morning would come much too quickly, and we had an adventure of the lifetime ahead of us when dawn came.

***

To travel to the DEEPEST PART OF THE FOREST, *turn to page 27*.
To SCALE THE CLIFF, *turn to page 21*.

UNDER THE WALL

"Neither are ideal, but swimming is probably the safer option," I said.

"I hid some supplies a while back for when I escaped." Axen removed a loose rock from the wall and pulled out an old crate. Inside lay a scraggly rope and a piece of parchment. They didn't look like they would be much help. "We'll use the rope to keep together. The currents under the wall can be pretty strong."

Axen tucked the parchment inside his jacket, tied one end of the rope around his waist and tossed the other end to me. I secured it around my middle as best I could.

"How far do we have to swim?" I asked.

"We should only need to be under water for a little over a minute. But we'll have to move fast. Let's go."

Axen led the way down the dark tunnel. The sound of water splashing against the rocks grew as we walked. Soon we were up to our knees in what I assumed was the edge of the ocean. Wading further in, Axen stopped for a moment to tighten our ropes.

"Swim down so you don't hit your head on the bottom of the wall, then follow me up to shore," he said from the darkness. "Ready?"

"I guess," I said, regretting every decision leading me to this moment.

Before I could think, Axen plunged under water tugging me with him. I swam as fast as I could after him. The deeper I swam, the stronger the currents lashed out. I hit my hand against the bottom of the wall and swam lower.

Just as I cleared the wall, an undercurrent hit me with full force, dragging me away from Axen. The water invaded my lungs, and I panicked as I struggled to breathe. I felt my consciousness dissipating when the rope around my waist tightened further, pulling me from the current's clutch. My weak grasp latched onto Axen's arm. Seconds later, we both broke through the glass ceiling of the sea. Crawling onto the beach, I coughed and gasped before lying down on the sand.

"Thank you," I said to Axen once I regained composure.

"Of course." Axen untied the rope from his waist.

After I purged my lungs of water, my mouth dried from the salt. Taking a few deep breaths, I stood and tried to brush the wet sand from my clothes. My waterlogged boots sank deeper in the sand unlike the security of the cobblestone and brick of Ashkelan.

After removing the soggy rope, I took in my surroundings. The beach stretched as far as I could see, the tide splashing against the rocky cliffs that separated the white sands from the lush forests above. The world was much bigger than I had ever dreamed.

"I thought the outside world was gone?" I looked at Axen who seemed unfazed by the beauty and vastness spread before us. "We were always taught that only a wasteland stretched beyond the wall."

"Keeping people in would be much harder if they knew the truth."

Before I could respond, I heard shouting from above. Two of the Answers' guards stood on top of the wall.

"Stop! You are fugitives from the law!"

As they clamored down a narrow stairway on the outside of the wall, Axen sprinted past me, barely grabbing my wrist to pull me along.

"Run!" he said as he released my arm and continued down the beach.

I tripped as I tried to gain footing in the uneven sand. I forced my legs to hold and took off after Axen at full speed, glancing back to see the guards hot on our trail. They didn't seem to mind the new terrain as much as I did. Clearly, they had been outside the wall before. I looked ahead in time to see Axen turn a bend and duck into a crevice in the cliff wall. I followed, the guards rushing past our hiding spot.

"Stay quiet." The air almost dissolved his hushed words before I heard them.

Staying quiet had never been my strong suit, especially now that every time I stayed still, the voices would start up their banter. *You're a fugitive now. You can never go home. Not that there was much of a home to go to.* I shut my eyes and leaned against the rocky mountain. After what seemed like hours, though was surely only moments, the guards walked past again, heading toward the outer wall. Once their voices had gone with the wind, I slid out of our hiding space.

"Now what?" I turned as Axen followed me out into the sunlight.

"Now, we find the camp of the readers. They will know what to do." Axen started down the beach again, leaving me to follow. Walking along the shore made my senses dizzy. The salty air assaulted my nose, and the ocean breeze whipped my dark hair from its braid. I shielded my eyes from the blazing sun and listened to the crashing waves that foamed around my feet.

Axen rounded another bend, and we came face to face with a cavern in the side of the cliffs. "This way," Axen said as he headed into the massive expanse. I followed behind, hesitant to leave the warm sun. The farther in we traveled, the bigger the cave appeared. The echoes of the waves, mixed with a stagnant smell, made for an eerie atmosphere. "We're almost to the entrance. Let me do the talking."

"Are we in danger?"

"Possibly."

My eyes widened as I saw a small gate up ahead, lit by a single lantern. Almost invisible against the rocks, the tall metal gate stood twice my height. As we approached, the metal bars in the center of the gate clanged open to reveal the face of a young man.

"Who are you?" he called.

"We're friends." Axen raised his hands in a position of surrender. "We're looking for refuge. We are readers and fugitives from the Answers."

The man eyed us with suspicion. "You may enter, but you may not stay without the blessing of our leader." The gate scraped open, and we walked into an underground paradise. The walls were lined with lanterns, their reflections sparkling in a creek running across the outskirts of a small village. The houses were little, and the roads dirt, but the whole town held an air of hominess. The people milling about seemed to freeze as we walked in, alarmed by intruders. An old man hobbled in our direction.

"Who are these newcomers, Lyden?" the elder asked the guard.

"They seek our protection, sir. They claim to be readers." Lyden stepped back and returned to his post by the gate.

"What are your names?" the old man asked.

"I'm Axen, and this is Calessa," Axen stated, his hands slightly raised in surrender.

"I see." The old man squinted at us from under bushy white eyebrows. His hunched postured relied on a knobby cane to keep him upright. "What do you know of the Final Answer?"

The Final Answer? I was about to voice my confusion when Axen jumped in.

"The Final Answer is the one sentence that could reverse the brainwashing done by the Answers. It is the only way to return the world to its original state."

I turned to him with my mouth agape. How did he know all of that?

"I see you can be trusted." The old man smiled. "My name is Aldred, and I am the leader of this village, the first refuge for readers. Come, have some food and water."

Aldred led us to a small hut built of wood and dirt. Inside, he motioned for us to sit at a table and brought us a plate of dried fruit and fresh vegetables. I munched quietly while I gazed around the musty room. A small shelf lined with books caught my eye, and I felt drawn to the words I knew were inside.

Aldred followed my gaze to the books. "I see you are a new reader."

"How could you tell?"

"Because of the way your eyes lit up when you saw my library. Only those who have just learned the power of words look at a simple book with that much desire."

I looked back at my food, unsure of how to respond. *What power? These voices? Stop. Shush. Not now.* "Yes," I managed to whisper, "I just learned I could read earlier today."

"Don't believe a thing you've heard." Aldred shook his finger at me. "Reading is a wonderful gift to have, you wait and see. But now, on to more important matters. It is quite a godsend that you two turned up here today. I am in need of some help. You see, the villagers and I are aging and cannot go out as we used to. I am sure some of the other camps have found clues to the final answer by now. I am just in need of some strong youngsters such as yourself to travel to their bases. Would you help us?" Aldred leaned forward in his chair, eyes expectant.

Axen turned to me and with a small nod, I confirmed we agreed. "Absolutely," I said. "We can't go home, so we might as well be of some help to someone."

"I agree. Where would you like us to go?" Axen faced Aldred.

"I have a map to the next camp. Once there, let them know I sent you. They will know who I am. There are two ways to get there. You can choose to go through a tunnel that leads you into the thickest part of the forest, or you can go back the way you came and take the long way around the side of this cliff. But no rush to decide tonight. Get some rest, and we will get you ready in the morning. And thank you. This means the world to me and my people ... our people."

Aldred set up some cots and gave us blankets to keep us warm in the damp chill of the cavern air.

That night as I tried to go to sleep, the voices spoke in whispers. *I hope you know what you're doing. This is turning into much more than you could ever have dreamed.* And with that, I drifted off to sleep, knowing morning would come much too quickly.

***

To travel to the DEEPEST PART OF THE FOREST, *turn to page 27.*
To take the LONG WAY AROUND, *turn to page 33.*

SCALE THE CLIFF—PRIDE AND PREJUDICE

"Now, where is the map you already have?" Aldred glanced at Axen as he went about packing for our trip.

Axen looked alarmed. "How did you know I had a map?"

"You had to find the entrance to this village somehow. I don't believe for a second you just stumbled upon it."

"Fair enough." Axen pulled the grimy paper from his jacket and laid it on the table. "Here. Though it cuts off at the entrance. It looks like it was torn from a larger map."

"That is correct, son. There once were detailed maps of all the realms, but they were destroyed little by little as the Answers found them. I only have the adjoining piece. I will pray the following camp will have another part for you."

Aldred walked to his bookshelf and pulled a folded piece of parchment from between the pages of an ancient-looking novel. When laid next to Axen's, the map now included the woods above the cliffs.

I traced my fingers along the edges of the map, and I saw in my mind what might lay beyond. *But how is it possible to see what is not there?* I blinked a few times and the visions disappeared. My heart racing, I tried to push the moment away and turned to Aldred. "You said there are other realms. What are they like?"

"They are all different and yet, the same." Aldred grabbed a small jar from a nearby shelf. "Some have magic and danger. Others are more peaceful. You never know quite what a realm is like until you have been there. Sadly, I have not traveled as much I would have liked." Opening the jar, he used a knife to smear a grimy substance onto the edge of our map. Pressing the new addition onto it, the two papers stuck together creating a single diagram of the world that I now desperately wanted to see.

"How many realms are there? Are they all as big as these woods?" Questions popped out of my mouth without warning.

"There are far too many realms for any one person to know. However, as for the size of these lands, they say some only take a half hour to walk from one to the other while others hold a month's worth of steps."

Shocked silent, I stared at the sketched parchment. Breaking the silence and my trance, Axen folded the map and placed it in his beaten leather jacket. "It's time for us to leave."

His eyes flashed with energy as they had done the day before. *I think Axen may know more than he is letting on.* For the first time, the voices in my head came as less of a shock. Perhaps I would get used to them after all.

Aldred and Axen packed supplies and food into a sack for Axen to carry on his back. My mind spun as we said our goodbyes and headed to the outskirts of the village.

"I think we should scale the cliffs. It will be safer than coming up in the middle of the woods unaware of our surroundings." Axen looked at me.

"Whatever you say is best."

I followed him back through the hidden door to the open beach. We walked closer to the city, tracing our steps from the chase the day before. Hugging the cliffs, I kept my eyes on the wall of Ashkelan. My heart pounded. I scanned the top of the wall for guards. A short walk later, we found a section of the rocky wall that seemed indented enough to conceal two fugitives trying to reach the top.

"Here looks good." Axen dropped his bag and rooted through it. Standing, he took a grapple-hook-ended rope and swung it above his head. Once the rope gained momentum, he let the metal fly toward the top of the cliff. It snagged in the jagged rocks above. After tugging to ensure the ropes were secured, Axen tied one rope around his middle to create a harness of sorts. Following his lead, I did the same.

"Do you know anything about the realms we're headed to?" I asked Axen as we tightened our ropes.

"Not really."

"All right. Well, do you think the next camp will have part of the Final Answer?"

"No clue."

I started another question but stopped. Either Axen wasn't a morning person, or he wasn't one to talk and climb at the same time. I stayed quiet and let Axen take the lead. The silence remained uncomfortable as we ascended toward an unknown world above. The climb started out easier than the one the day before. Having a little experience must go a long way in activities such as this. The climb still seemed grueling and painful, but I trusted I would make it to the top with fewer battle scars than from yesterday's hurried escape.

As we neared the top, I heard a low rumble coming from above. Finding my next foothold, I stopped. "Do you hear that?"

"Yes." Axen stopped and tilted his head, listening intently. "Be careful, it sounds like the rocks above us are shifting."

Moving slowly, Axen and I traveled farther, but with every move the rumble grew louder. We were only about three feet from the top when the voices interrupted my concentration. *You need to stop climbing. You're going to cause a rockslide. You could be killed.* I brushed off the warning. What did I know about cliff anatomy anyway? Grabbing the rope higher, I planted my foot in a crevice and pulled. The noise became almost deafening. I looked up to see the rocks our grapples were hooked on give way.

"Axen!" I yelled as I let the rope go and clung to the cliff wall. Thankfully, Axen did the same. Both of us were showered in rocks and debris as a full-blown rockslide pummeled us. The mountain didn't seem to care whether we lived or died. I waited for a fatal blow to the head, but one never came. I heard a yell and looked over to see Axen had not been as lucky. A stone had created a gash above his eyebrow. The blow could have been much worse—at least he was conscious. The blood dripped into his eyes as he seethed through the pain. As quick as it started, the rockslide ended. All that remained above us were craggy rocks and dirt leading to the top.

"Are you all right?" I said watching Axen wipe the blood from his eyes.

"I'm fine. Get to the top."

Not having our ropes tethered made for a dangerous turn of events as we had to climb without any provisions of safety. But with his anger and pain evident, Axen fought his way up the mountain.

I followed, reaching for only the safest of holds along the way. As I neared the top, however, one hold proved not to be as safe as I believed. My hand slid right through the soft earth causing another shower of dust and mud to rain onto me. I gasped as my feet slipped from their ledge, and I dangled by one hand. I could feel the rocks giving way as I reached with desperation for anything solid. I managed to grab hold to a secure rock and regained my balance with only seconds to spare. Reaching the top, I pulled myself up onto solid ground and looked around. The sea lay behind us, the Ashkelan wall to our right, and, stretching beyond, a forest of epic proportions. Axen was on his knees rummaging through his bag.

"Here, let me help you," I said.

"I don't need help."

"Axen, you're bleeding. Let me help." I pulled the bag away from him and found the bandages we'd packed. I had hoped we wouldn't need to use them, especially not this close to the start of our journey. Axen's eyes flickered with pain as I used water from our canteen to wash his wound and wrapped the bandages around his head. Finished with my makeshift doctoring, I stood and brushed off what dirt I could from my pants and scanned the woods ahead. "Which way do we go?"

Axen studied the map. "This way."

He walked toward the trees, and I again had no choice but to follow. Shortly after we entered the woods, a delicious aroma awoke our hunger. Following our noses, we entered a clearing with several tents strewn about and a handful of people huddled around a small fire, roasting some sort of animal. Our approach startled them, and before we could react, we were face to face with three men armed with swords.

Axen emerged from the tree line. "Wait! Please. Don't hurt us, we're friends. We came from the base camp."

One of the men lowered his weapon and stepped up to confront us. "How can we be sure?"

"Look at the map Aldred gave us, which shows your exact location. We were sent to see if you have found the Final Answer." Axen unfolded the map and let the men take their time looking at it. Soon enough, they lowered their swords and invited us to join them for lunch.

"We don't have the Final Answer." The same man who confronted us spoke as we ate, and the women of the camp attended to Axen's injury. "However," he continued, "We believe we may have found a clue." He entered one of the tents and returned a moment later holding a book. "We found this copy of a classic novel a while back, and while reading, we noticed one part underlined."

After opening the book to the marked page, he handed it to Axen. Moving closer, I saw the underlined phrase. The letters swirled again into words as I read. "'What are men to rocks and mountains?'" I read aloud. My mind turned to the rockslide, playing it through my mind as if reliving it.

"What does it mean?"

"We're not sure how it's connected, but this book was one of the original copies owned by the author herself. There must be a reason she pointed out that exact line."

"Well, I guess that's a start." I took the book from Axen and closed it to see the cover: *Pride and Prejudice* by Jane Austen.

"It is." Axen stood and turned to the man. "But we need to keep moving. Do you know how far to the next camp?"

The man disappeared yet again into the tent, returning with a piece of parchment. "Here is another piece of the map. It will lead you to the next camp. It's about a three-hour trek from here." The man traced his finger along faded lines. "You can either go through this valley that connects to the woods or go down through the woods themselves. We have not traveled there, or we would tell you which is the better choice." The man attached the new piece to our existing one.

"Well," Axen turned to me, "which way do you want to go?"

***

To go THROUGH THE VALLEY, *turn to page 41.*
To go THROUGH THE WOODS, *turn to page 47.*

DEEPEST PART OF THE FOREST—1984

"Here is the portion of the map I have." Aldred spread a piece of parchment out on the table. "You must have another part of the map if you found this camp. Where is it?"

"Here." Axen pulled the map from his jacket and Aldred laid the pieces together.

"Now, as I said, this is only a portion of the full map of the realms. I pray the other camps will have more to add." Aldred traced his hands over the beach and woods that were drawn on the map.

"Realms?" I asked.

"Yes. Some are small, others would take months to cross. Each has its own climate, terrain, and dangers."

"I see." My mind envisioned the possibilities of what may lay ahead. *Wait. How am I seeing what may not even be real?* The voices were interrupted by Axen.

"I think the tunnel is our best option for reaching the next camp." Axen stood over the map while Aldred packed supplies for our trip. "It will be the easiest way to stay hidden." He folded the map and placed it in his pocket. Soon after, Aldred walked Axen and me to a far corner of the village.

"The entrance to the tunnel is there." Aldred pointed to a section of the cavern with a break in the wall. "Be sure you find light. Those tunnels leave little room for the sun. Good luck, young ones. I hope you find our answer." The old man turned and returned to his home as Axen and I turned toward the start of what promised to be a long day.

Reaching the opening, Axen grabbed a torch from the bag he held on his back and lit it. Mumbling something about watching my step, he entered the dark hole. Following cautiously, I took his advice and watched as the ground became uneven as we walked. The low glow of the torch gave off only enough light to see three steps ahead at a time.

After following the tunnel straight for a while, my mind began to get antsy in the quiet. "Do you know any more about the Final Answer?" I asked Axen.

"Not really."

"Well, what about the voices? Can you tell me more about them?"

"Not really."

I realized I was probably not going to get much more of an answer, so I chose to embrace the peace while we had it. Who knew what might lay ahead?

Not long after, the tunnel came to an opening that branched out in multiple directions.

"Which way do we go?" I looked at Axen as he pulled the map from his pocket.

"I'm not sure. The map doesn't show the specifics of the tunnel. Only the general direction. We'll have to guess. The torch is about to go out too, so we need to decide quick." Axen put the map away and started to examine the various openings.

You're going to get lost down here with no light. You might as well give up and turn around. The voices bombarded my mind as I stared at the dying flame. My breath quickened, and I felt my head start to grow fuzzy.

"Calessa, don't freak out on me now. We need to keep moving. This way." Axen moved toward the center tunnel.

Before I could take a step, the dizziness took control, and I crumpled to the floor of the cave.

"Calessa!"

Axen dropped to my side while I watched the last of the light die out. We were plunged into darkness. The clammy air crawled on my skin as I struggled to see. I clung to Axen as he sat next to me on the damp floor.

"I'm sorry," I whispered.

"It's okay. We'll have to try to feel our way through the tunnel."

Axen helped me stand but the darkness was far beyond what my eyes could adjust to. Stumbling forward a few steps, I reached for Axen's arm. As I did, I caught the slightest glimmer of light from the corner of my eye. I walked blindly toward it, shuffling my feet to avoid tripping on any protruding rocks.

"Axen, do you see this?" The closer I got, I realized there was not just one source of light, but hundreds. Scattered around the entrance of the farthest tunnel were tiny flecks of luminescent minerals. Looking deeper into the tunnel revealed the walls were lined with thousands of these sparkling gems, creating a warm, rosy glow. "I think we should use this tunnel. At least there is some light to help us find our way."

"Okay, let's go then." Axen started into the glimmering tunnel.

I followed close behind and stared in wonder at the beauty that came once the luminescence took over. Following the light, we soon reached a mossy opening between the roots of a tree. Climbing back onto the topsoil, I looked around to see nothing but green in every direction. Trees surrounded us with little to see in between. Axen didn't take any time for a rest as he pulled out his map and turned toward the forest.

"The camp should be in this direction. Let's go."

I took a few deep breaths of the fresh air and followed Axen into the woods. The trees made a canopy that blocked most of the daylight, making it hard to keep track of time as we walked. My stomach rumbled, and I assumed it was already near mid-day.

The quiet of the forest was only interrupted by the occasional bird call, the scurrying of a squirrel, and the crack of twigs under our feet. *Maybe this trip won't be so bad.*

The closeness of the mountainous trees caused many scratches and bruises from stray branches and rough bark. My energy diminished as my hunger grew, and from looking at Axen, I assumed he felt the same. Our steps slowed and we made frequent stops to breathe and double check the map. After another hour of twig stomping and bird calls, a new sound disturbed the peace. Voices carried through the trees.

"Keep quiet." Axen snuck closer to the voices, and I watched my steps to keep from causing any unneeded sounds. The voices grew louder and with them the smell of something wonderful teased my senses. My stomach growled, and I clamped a hand over it, hoping the sound was quieter than it felt. Nearing the edge of the tree line, I could see the camp spread out in a clearing. Tents were strewn about, and occupants huddled around a fire near the center. The wonderful smell emanated from a large kettle balanced over the flames.

I looked to Axen for some signal of what to do next, and he motioned us forward. Walking closer to the camp, I kept an eye on my companion. He stared at the group of men and women around the fire. With both of our attentions drawn away from the forest floor, neither of us saw the thin line of string that had been rigged between two trees. Next thing I knew, we had tripped over their simple trap and were sprawled on the ground. The breath left my lungs as I landed hard on the ground. All hopes of staying undetected vanished.

The men of the camp scrambled to their feet and turned to face us, swords at the ready. "Who goes there?" one shouted.

Axen and I stood as the men surrounded us.

"Please. Wait." Panic filled my voice as their silver blades glinted in the sun. "We came from the base camp. Aldred sent us. He gave us a map that led us here. We came to see about the Final Answer." I spoke quickly, leaving myself no time to breathe in between words.

The men lowered their weapons. "I see. And who are you exactly?" The same man who had yelled now stepped forward as leader of the pack.

Axen had regained composure and stood by my side. "I'm Axen. This is Calessa."

"Well, welcome to our camp." The man motioned for us to join them around the fire. "Anyone sent by Aldred is trusted here. Though I am not sure I have much good news in way of the Final Answer."

"So, you don't have anything to help us?" Disappointment laced my words.

"We don't have the answer in its entirety. However, I do believe we may have a clue. Wait here." The man disappeared into a tent and returned a moment later with an ancient book and a piece of parchment. "This book was found quite a while ago, and while reading, I noticed one part had been underlined. Seeing that it is an original copy from the author, I know it must mean something. Here." He opened the book and handed it to us.

Looking at the page, my mind swirled the letters together to form words once again. "'We shall meet in the place where there is no darkness.'" My mind returned to our trip through the glowing tunnel. Somewhat stunned by the connection, I closed the book and saw the title and byline: *1984* by George Orwell.

"What do you think it means?" I asked.

"We aren't sure. But I know it must be important." The man took the book from our hands and started to unfold the parchment he had brought. "I also have a map that may help you locate the next camp."

Axen took the map and unfolded ours next to it. The woods expanded on the new piece, showing more of our ever-growing world. A large ravine stretched beside the woods. On the other side was a mark that showed the location of the next camp.

"Which path is safer?" Axen asked.

"We don't know," the man said. "The last scout we sent out never returned. You can try the ravine, or you can brave the forest to stay hidden. Either way will have its trials."

Axen looked at me. "Well? Which way do you think we should go?"

***

To go THROUGH THE WOODS, *turn to page* 47

To go THROUGH THE RAVINE, *turn to page* 53

THE LONG WAY AROUND—ANNE OF GREEN GABLES

"Have you decided which way you will go?" Aldred asked as he helped us prepare for our trip. He loaded a satchel with supplies and food as Axen and I ate a light breakfast and mulled over our map.

"I think it would be best to take the long way around. It may take longer, but I would rather not risk our lives in some tunnel." Axen looked to Aldred. "You said you had another piece of the map?"

"Ah, yes." The elderly man walked to a shelf and pulled an old book from its place. Pulling a piece of parchment from between the pages, he laid it next to our current one. The world expanded as the woods above the beach were put into full view. "This only shows the realm of the forest. The rest of the world is but a mystery even to me."

My fingers traced the edge of the parchment. "How much more is there?"

"We may never know." Aldred looked wistfully at the sketched lines in front of him. "The world is made of many realms. Some may be small or harmless while others could be a large as an ocean or as dangerous as an erupting volcano.

I didn't get to see near as much of the world as I had wanted to in my youth."

My eyes widened as I visualized the monstrous world that may await us. *How am I seeing things I have never known?* The voices, now a normality, created a wave of confusion. I stared at the map, trying to make sense of what I saw in my mind.

"We should be on our way," Axen said, breaking my trance. He folded the map and placed it in his pocket. Then, he gathered our things and shouldered the satchel of supplies, leaving me to dawdle behind him in a haze. Aldred led us back to the entrance we had located the day before.

"Stay close to the cliffs to avoid being spotted by any guards," Aldred warned. "And remember, tell the members of the next camp who sent you. It is the only way they will know you can be trusted." He turned to return to his village as we walked back toward the beach.

"Do you know anything about the realms he talked about?" I asked.

"No." Axen kept his eyes forward.

"Well, what do you think about the Final Answer? Do you think we'll find it?"

"I don't know."

The more time I spent in Axen's presence, the more confused I became. One moment, he seemed thoughtful, and the next, he came across cold and calculated like a machine. I followed his lead in silence as we stepped into the morning sun. Hugging the cliffs gave us little shade to ward off the heat, but I was thankful to at least be hidden from the view of the Ashkelan wall. We retraced our steps from the chase the day before and then continued around the side of the cliffs.

Sooner than I would have liked, we came face to face with the wall as the cliffs met the stony exterior. From the base, we couldn't see the top, but I could hear the voices of men patrolling the perimeter. Axen didn't need to remind me to be quiet as we crept closer to the wall.

We turned to see that a worn path had been beaten into the ground next to the city. The trail led straight from the beach up the side of the cliffs in an easy grade, all the way to the edge of the forest above.

"This way." Axen started up the trail. "Stay close." We stayed low to the ground as we traveled closer to the woods. A voice from above startled us, and we flattened ourselves against the wall, praying we wouldn't be spotted. The voice trailed off and we continued our trek. Reaching the edge of the woods, we ducked behind the wall of trees. Breathing deep for the first time since the climb, I sat against the roots and tried to calm my beating heart.

Axen must not have needed much of a break since he stayed still for only a moment before starting through the forest. I glanced up at the sky to see that it was already mid-day or better based on the position of the sun. The climb up must have taken longer than I thought.

"We need to keep moving." Axen was already way ahead of me and I scrambled to my feet to follow.

"I'm getting hungry," I said as my stomach began to protest.

Axen kept walking. "It's too soon to waste our provisions."

What seemed like forever passed as we walked through the rough forest, gaining minor wounds from the branches. My body weakened from hunger, and finally, I collapsed onto the forest floor.

"Axen, please. We have to eat something."

Axen grunted his displeasure at the delay and then walked to an area crowded with bushes and greenery of all kinds. He returned with a handful of bright orange berries for each of us.

"If we eat off the land, we avoid using our supplies. Hopefully, this will hold us." He popped his berries in his mouth all at once. The sour tang of the juice hit my tongue as I ate my portion slowly, savoring each of the tiny fruits. I was only about halfway through my snack when a loud yell erupted from Axen.

"Ah! Get back!" Axen flung his arms like crazy. "Calessa, watch out!"

I looked around but nothing seemed out of the ordinary. "What are you talking about?"

"The wasps! Don't you see the wasps? They're everywhere! Watch your step, they're covering the ground!" Axen looked like a lunatic as he pranced around avoiding whatever invisible insects he saw.

"Axen, calm down! There aren't any wasps!" I tried to grab his arm only to have his hand fly back and catch me in the mouth. I fell to the ground cupping my bleeding lip as I watched my crazed companion. He continued his manic episode and I tried to make sense of it.

He's hallucinating! The berries ... oh no ... you ate them too. The voices were interrupted as my mind turned fuzzy, and my brain fought off the effects of the poison invading my system. I started to see little flickers of movement around me. The wasps. I saw them now. I batted them away, but my hand moved through their nonexistent bodies. *Calm down, Calessa, they aren't real. No! They are here, I can see them. Calm down, they are only in your mind. Shut your eyes and breathe.* I listened to the voices and closed my eyes. I heard the buzzing of the wasps and Axen's yells, but somehow, was able to calm myself.

I opened my eyes and noticed the wasps, while still there and buzzing, seemed less clear. Their bodies seemed to glitch through the air, and the buzzing became monotone and steady. I evened my breathing and stood, forcing myself to walk straight toward Axen and not bothering to dodge the wasps. I grabbed him by the shoulders and turned him to face me. His eyes looked panicked and blitzed with an electric current.

"Axen, listen to me. They aren't real. I need you to trust me."

Axen seemed close to hyperventilating, and I knew I needed

to get him out of there fast before he collapsed. I pulled the map from his pocket and opened it. My eyes had trouble focusing, and my mind still blurred as I tried to ignore the buzzing.

"We need to go this way." I started to pull Axen along.

He followed, though clearly, he was far from present in that moment. After a while, I felt Axen start to drag behind me. It took all my strength to keep us standing as I pushed forward toward the camp. After what seemed like days, I saw the edge of the trees ahead. I could make out tents and people gathered around a fire. *There's the camp. Only a little farther.* The voices propelled me forward though my mind and body were exhausted with the after effects of the poisonous fruit. I didn't even bother to stay quiet as I neared the edge of the camp. The men of the camp heard the commotion and stood, swords at their sides. Fully supporting Axen, I trudged out from the trees.

One of the men stepped forward and bared his sword. "Who are you?"

"Aldred—"

***

I woke to the hushed voices of the members of the camp. I sat up, my mind groggy, and looked around. I was in a large tent. To my right, Axen lay on a cot—still out cold. The same man who had spoken earlier approached me.

"Are you all right?" he asked.

"I think so." I tried to stand, but the wooziness forced me to sit back down. "Is Axen okay?"

"I'm assuming that's your traveling companion." The man walked over to Axen's cot. "I think he will be fine. Did you two get into some bad berries by chance?"

"Yes, we did." I rubbed my pounding head.

"You passed out before explaining yourself, but I did hear you say the name Aldred. Do you know him?"

"Yes, we came from the base camp. My name is Calessa and that's Axen. We were sent to see if you had the Final Answer."

"Ah, we do not have the answer, but we may have a clue to help you. But first, let's get you something better to eat and wait for Axen to wake up."

Soon after, Axen rejoined the world, and we all sat around a table, eating much better food than we had found in the woods.

"Now, about the Final Answer." The man of the camp held an ancient book in his hands. "I found this original copy of Anne of Green Gables by Lucy Maud Montgomery. While I was reading, I noticed the author had underlined one specific line." He opened the book and handed it to me.

Looking down, I watched letters swirl like they had in the library, and I began to see the words before me. "'When you are imagining, you might as well imagine something worthwhile.'"

That's funny. Imagining. Is that like the hallucinations? It does remind me of when I saw the realms of the map before knowing they were there. The voices spoke in bursts as I tried to make sense.

"We don't know how it is connected to the Final Answer, but it has to mean something." The man stood, retrieved a piece of parchment from between the pages of another book, and laid it out on the table. "Here is a section of a map that may help you find the next camp."

I pulled our map out and matched the edges to the new one. A ravine stretched next to the woods and a field covered another expanse. The next camp lay toward the other edge. "Which way should we go to reach it?" I asked.

"I'm not sure which is best. You can either travel through this ravine or stay on higher ground by going through this valley." The man traced two different paths.

Axen stood and spoke for the first time since awakening. "Thank you for your help, but we should keep moving." He folded up our map and looked at me. "Which way do you want to go?"

***

To GO THROUGH THE RAVINE, *turn to page* 53
To GO THROUGH THE FIELD, *turn to page* 59

***

THROUGH THE VALLEY—ROMEO
AND JULIET

"Let's go through the valley. It will probably be safe there."

Axen agreed and began packing our supplies.

"Thank you for your hospitality." I shook hands with the man who had helped us.

"Of course. Anything for a friend of Aldred's."

The ladies of the camp gave us some food for the road, and we said our goodbyes. Leaving the camp, we headed toward the outskirts of the woods. Thankfully, it didn't take too long to reach the edge of the forest.

Stepping out into the sun, my breath caught in my throat. The outside world looked more beautiful with every change of scenery. A stretch of grass led down into a soft valley of wildflowers and moss. The fragrant flowers infused the air with their scent making for a delightful aroma I could almost taste. The sun warmed my skin, and my hair wafted across my face from the gentle breeze. I had never felt this alive within the walls of Ashkelan.

"I wonder if the whole world is as beautiful as this."

"I'm sure there are plenty of realms that aren't near as nice." Axen started walking down into the valley.

41

"Maybe." I sighed. "But I bet they have their beautiful parts too." Axen snorted, and I took his displeasure as a sign to change the subject. "What was it like to be in Answers Headquarters?"

"You won't want to hear it."

"Maybe not, but it might be good to talk about it."

"I'd rather not. Can't you leave it alone?"

I took the cue and stopped talking. As we walked into the valley, my boots sank a little into the mossy ground. Leaning down, I picked a few flowers, trying to occupy the voices in my head to keep them quiet. Soon, we were deep in the valley, too deep to see the woods we had come from or the end we were looking for. The sun started on a rapid descent and my body began to tire.

"Axen, do you think we could rest for a while?"

"No, we need to reach the camp before dark."

"All right." I kept trudging along, my limbs starting to feel like jelly. The sky changed colors, and I stared in wonder as pinks and purples collided with the bright orange of the setting sun. The vivid scene melded into the green like a rainbow without the rain.

The air cooled as the sun hid itself behind the walls of the valley, and the shadows danced their way to bed as dusk fell. I could see the end of the valley was still too far off to make before dark.

"We need to keep moving." Axen walked farther into the darkening path.

"We aren't going to make it before dark."

"Doesn't matter. We keep walking."

I followed silently, feeling as if Axen was still upset with me over the questions from earlier. I busied myself by watching the sky as the colors faded to a soft black and the stars began to shine. In Ashkelan, there are too many lights for the stars to be seen. *I remember trying to count the stars. I thought twenty in one night seemed incredible. Now I'm looking at thousands.* The voices brought up memories of lying in the central courtyard, squinting to see past the streetlights. I blinked back tears and hushed the voices.

Instead, I focused on Axen as he walked down the valley, lost in his own mind. *I wonder what his voices say to him.*

The voices continued their incessant chatter as I looked back to the sky. I watched the moon move with the stars trailing along. *Shouldn't they be going the other way?* My mind raced for a moment and I stopped. Looking ahead, and through the dark, I could barely make out the end of the valley which hadn't gotten any closer even though we had been walking for quite a while. I looked back at the sky and tried to catch up to Axen who walked at a much faster pace. The moon slid farther along the velvety black sky in the opposite direction it should. The end of the valley was getting farther away rather than closer.

"Axen, stop!"

"No, I've already told you. We keep going."

"No, Axen, stop! Look! The end is getting farther away. The stars are moving in reverse. Something isn't right."

Axen stopped and looked up. I caught up to him, though it made no difference on the distance we had yet to travel.

"I guess I wasn't paying attention." Axen rubbed the back of his neck. "I still think we should keep going."

"And what? End up just as far from the end as when we started? If not farther?" I scowled at Axen. "We're staying here."

"What if it doesn't go back to normal in the morning? Then what?"

"Then we deal with that then. But for now, I'm tired and hungry, and I say we're staying here." I pulled the bag off Axen's back and sat down to sort through the food we had brought from the camp.

"Fine, but we need to get an early start." Axen sat next to me and portioned out the food.

After eating, we pulled two small blankets from the bag and used them as makeshift pillows. The warm air kept us from being chilled, and my exhausted body had no trouble drifting off to sleep.

Axen shook me awake after what seemed like only moments. The sun peeking over the valley edge proved it must have been longer.

"I think we're safe now. I walked a few feet down this path and the sun stayed on its course." Axen had already packed up his blanket and was ready to go.

I stifled a yawn as I spoke. "That's good."

We started off again and Axen had been right. The end of the valley was getting closer now, though we still had at least an hour's walk left. The new day brought the familiar smells and sounds from the day before, and the beginning of our journey seemed far from terrible. A comfortable silence fell over us, and I felt content with the solitude until Axen stopped and turned.

"Do you smell that?" His nose wrinkled in disgust.

I took a deep breath and almost gagged. Something smelled rotten, ruining the dainty scent of the flowers. "What is that?"

"I'm not sure." Axen took a few steps forward. "It's definitely coming from up ahead."

I took shallow breaths and held my nose as we moved along. The smell became almost unbearable. Axen stopped again and pointed to the side of the valley.

"I think that's the source of the smell."

I followed his finger and almost screamed. A human body, covered in bugs and dirt, lie dead on the floor of the valley. I tried to ask questions, but they caught in my throat and I turned away.

"He doesn't look hurt." I heard Axen move around the body. "I'm not sure what killed him."

"Maybe it was the delayed time?" The voices created a million scenarios in my head.

"Maybe. Hey, look here. He has something in his pocket."

I forced myself to turn around and walk closer to Axen as he unfolded two sheets of paper. One had traces of writing, though most of the marks were smudged off. *Always ... morning ... I wonder what that means.* The other paper showed a map much like the one we were following to reach the camp. *I wonder if he was from the next camp.*

Axen seemed unfazed by the clues and tucked them in his jacket before continuing down the path. I whispered a prayer for the deceased and kept moving. Reaching the end of the valley, we headed up the hill. A small village sat off in the distance and we started our way toward it. When we'd drawn closer, a lady came out to meet us.

"What can I do for you?" She squinted at us but seemed friendly.

"We were sent by Aldred," I said. "He sent us to see about the Final Answer."

"Oh my, I guess our scout never made it." Her hand went to her mouth and she frowned. "I was starting to worry, and I thought about sending someone after him. Oh, I wonder where he is."

"Ma'am," Axen interrupted her stream of thoughts. I was glad he chose to break the news rather than me. "I think we came across your scout on our way here. I'm sorry, ma'am, but he didn't make it."

"Oh." The woman's stare went blank as she processed the news. "We sent him out about a week ago. I never would've thought the valley could've killed someone. We even sent him at night so he might avoid any trouble."

Axen and I exchanged glances, knowing that was probably the reason he had ended up dead.

The lady wiped away a tear that had escaped her eye and shook her head. "No use crying about it now. You two are here for the answer, and I might have something that will help. Come with me."

We followed the lady back to her home, and she gave us breakfast while she scurried about looking for whatever she had for us. Soon, she returned to the table with a book in hand.

"This here is an original copy of *Romeo and Juliet* by William Shakespeare. The author underlined a quote, and I believe it may mean something to the Final Answer." The woman opened the book and slid it across the table for Axen and me to see.

"'That I shall say goodnight till it be morrow.'" I stifled a snort at the irony as Axen read the line aloud.

"I'm not sure of the connection, but it must've been important for the author himself to mark it." The woman took the book back and disappeared into another room for a moment. When she returned, she was holding a piece of parchment.

"I have a piece of a map here if you two need directions to the next camp."

She laid it out on the table and Axen pulled ours from his jacket. It lined up perfectly, showing a camp just north of our current location.

"It looks like a river runs straight to the camp." Axen pointed out a sketched pathway leading along a shade of blue.

"That's true," she said. "You can either go that way, or you can go through this mountain range here. It may take a little longer but will give you more coverage." She stood and started to gather some food from around her kitchen. "Here, let me restock your supplies while you decide."

***

To go ALONG THE RIVER, *turn to page 65*
To go THROUGH THE MOUNTAIN RANGE, *turn to page 71*

THROUGH THE WOODS—THE PICTURE OF DORIAN GREY

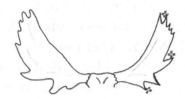

"Staying in the woods will keep us out of sight and out of the heat." I looked at Axen and he nodded.

"Good point." He stood and folded the map. "We should be on our way. I want to reach the next camp before nightfall."

The men of the camp helped Axen add some supplies to our load, and we said our goodbyes. A short while later we wandered through the dense forest, following our map as we went.

"It should only be a few hours' trek to the next camp as long as we keep moving forward at a decent pace. We'll stay there for the night."

I listened to Axen talk but was too enraptured to respond. The woods seemed like a magical place and my senses went wild with the experience. The smell of fresh rain wafted on a breeze that twirled my hair and made me smile. I heard a crunch and looked down at a vast sea of twigs and leaves scattering the forest floor. I picked up a leaf and twirled it between my finger, the sun glinting through the translucent sides. I closed my eyes and breathed deep. Fresh, invigorating air filled my lungs. I had never known anything but smog-filled city air, and now that I had tasted the outside, I was intoxicated.

I opened my eyes and scrambled to catch up to Axen. "Isn't this the most beautiful place you've ever seen?"

"Anything is better than Ashkelan." His eyes stared straight, untouched by emotion.

I wonder what happened to him. He must have been treated terribly at Answers Headquarters.

"What was it like being brainwashed and conscripted?"

He glanced at me and then focused on the trail ahead once more. "Terrible. I'm lucky I made it out when I did." Axen's expression never wavered as he spoke. I chose not to press any further. After all, I had only known him for two days. I needed to build some trust between us first.

As I tried to think of another topic to talk about, a horrible smell flooded the fresh air I had come to love.

I scrunched up my nose. "Do you smell that?"

Axen walked toward a dense section of trees. "Yes, it's coming from over here." After looking behind the trunk of one of the giants, he stepped back and put out his hand to stop my approach. "You don't want to come over here. I found the cause of the smell. There's a dead man here." He glanced back once at the offensive sight. "Seems he's been dead a few days by the looks and smell."

I chose to trust Axen on this one and stayed where I was. He knelt by the tree and reached toward something there. Soon, he returned to me with a small pouch in his hand.

"Something big must have gotten to him. He had gashes all through his chest, but he had this clutched in his hand." Opening the pouch, Axen pulled out a piece of a map. It indicated the camp we had come from as well as the camp we were headed to. The parchment had something written on the back and Axen turned it over to look. The pencil marks had been smudged away, but a single word stood out: define.

I stopped for a moment as the voices tried to figure out the meaning. I tried to shush them by listening for the sounds of the forest. The trees rustled in the wind, but, other than that, the woods had grown strangely quiet.

"Axen, does something seem off to you?"

He continued to scan the map. "Not really. Why?"

"Well, the birds aren't singing, and I don't see any squirrels or rabbits. They had been all around us a bit ago."

"Must be a quieter part of the for—"

A loud crash came from close by, shaking the ground. Axen pulled me behind a tree and put his finger to his lips. Another rumble echoed and I felt it in my feet. Something big was rampaging through the trees. I peeked around the trunk and stifled a scream. A creature, taller than Axen and I combined, crushed the leaves, sticks, and everything else in its path as it made toward us.

"What are we up against?" Axen whispered.

I tore my eyes away from the creature and back to Axen. "A ... a monster." My voice quivered as I spoke. "It's ... it's gigantic." Another crash caused me to sneak another glimpse. The thing seemed even larger now as it drew closer. "It has the head of a lion but the body and antlers of a deer. I've never seen any ... anything like it."

A giant hoof landed next to me as I tried to quiet my breathing. The foot alone was almost half my height. Tears threatened to fall as I looked up, praying the creature wouldn't see me. Drool dripped down from his jaw and his teeth were bared. His breath came down hot and heavy on me as I tried to stay as still as possible. The monster took another step forward, and I ducked to avoid being hit. After the front hoof had cleared my head and the creature had taken a few more steps away, I stood once more. When I did, a twig snapped under my boot. A small gasp escaped my lips, and the creature stopped in its tracks. The beast turned and speared me with a glare from the biggest eyes I had ever seen, black and flared with anger.

I choked on my tears as I tried to find my voice.

"Stay calm. Those antlers look sharp enough to kill."

A low growl emanated from the beast as he lowered his head. The antlers were thicker than the tree limbs and sharpened to points at the ends. *I could've sworn those antlers had been dull a moment ago.* My mind tried to comprehend how I could've missed such a major detail when a loud roar shook me back to reality. The monster charged. I ran. A loud yell told me Axen hadn't.

I looked back and saw an antler had skewered the tree I had been just standing behind. I stopped as the creature backed up, revealing a crumpled Axen holding his arm as blood seeped through his fingers. I noticed a flicker of fear go through the creature's eyes as Axen grabbed a rock from nearby. My companion raised his unharmed arm to throw the small boulder at the monster's head. The animal roared in protest and pawed the ground, reading to strike again.

"Wait! I think he's just scared. Don't threaten him."

Axen dropped the rock and the creature backed away a few steps.

"He almost killed us." Axen spoke through gritted teeth, his own eyes angrier than the beast's. "What do you expect to do? Talk to him?" He kept his glare on the monster.

"I think he's as scared of us as we are of him." The beast's fur quivered as it backed away further. "He only attacked because he thought we would hurt him. He really isn't as much of a monster as I thought." The beast's eyes softened, and I could see the muscles in his back release their tension.

"I still think we should kill him."

"No. We aren't killing an innocent creature. Look at him! He's trembling! He's not going to hurt us anymore." I took a step closer to the beast, and he jerked his head to look at me. Without the roars and the anger in his eyes, he seemed almost beautiful. "He's a pretty handsome creature when he's not trying to kill us."

What happened next could only be described as magic. The beast's fur lightened and smoothed. His antlers returned to the dull state I had first seen, and his mane grew fuller and softer. The creature took a tentative step toward me and lowered his head. I reached out. The beast leaned into me allowing my fingers to tangle in his soft mane.

Axen came and stood next to me, still eyeing the creature with distrust. Blood seeped from his wound. The creature's eyes softened with regret, lowering his head. Axen sighed and returned to our supplies. Giving the animal one last pat, I joined my companion. Axen handed me the first aid without a word. Sitting down, I wrapped his gash securely.

"He seemed to come out of nowhere," I pondered aloud. "It wouldn't surprise me if he disappeared just as quickly." I turned to look at our newfound friend, but he was nowhere to be seen. Apparently, it did surprise me. My jaw dropped. "Where did he go?"

"I don't know. But let's keep moving before something else decides to kill us."

We made our way through the rest of the forest with no more distractions and soon spotted a little village ahead that must have been the camp we sought. A woman came to greet us before we'd reached the edge of the village.

"Friends or enemies?" she asked.

"Friends," I said quickly. "We came from the base camp. Aldred sent us to find the Final Answer."

"Ah, well then, welcome. Let's get you two inside." The woman led us to a house in the village and immediately set to work on dressing Axen's wounds. "Did you two happen to come across a man on your travels? I believe we have a clue to the Final Answer, and I sent a scout to take it to the next camp."

Axen and I shared a glance and then he turned to her and spoke quietly. "I'm sorry, ma'am, but I think your scout may be dead. We found a body in the woods. He was holding this." Axen gave the pouch to the woman, who took it and sat down, staring at the small leather satchel.

"Yes, this was his." Her voice wavered. She cleared her throat, wiped her eyes, and then hurried to another room.

A while later, she returned with a book.

Having pulled herself together, she opened the book and pulled out a piece of parchment from inside. "I apologize for leaving so abruptly," she said. "That scout was a dear friend of mine."

I patted her shoulder. "It's all right."

"I believe this may be of some use to you." She handed me the book, *The Picture of Dorian Grey*. "The author of this book, Oscar Wilde, passed down this copy of his classic, and a single line is underlined. I think it may be important."

I opened the book to a page that had been marked and read the quote aloud. "'To define is to limit.'" The voices in my head started to calculate everything I had just experienced in the woods. *Like defining the monster. It only attacked when Axen said it was angry. And that would explain its disappearance too.*

The woman's voice snapped me out of my trance.

"This might also help." She had unfolded the parchment, revealing another piece of map to attach to our current one. "There are two trails that lead to the next camp to the north of here. You can either go through this mountain range here"— she pointed to the map—"or go across the lake to this side." She handed Axen the map and smiled. "But for now, I think you two need some food and some rest."

Neither of us disagreed. Soon, with full stomachs, we had settled in. I could only hope the next day would make a bit more sense than this one.

***

To go THROUGH THE MOUNTAIN RANGE, *turn to page 71*
To go ACROSS THE LAKE, *turn to page 77*

***

THROUGH THE RAVINE— WUTHERING HEIGHTS

"I guess we should go through the ravine." I looked at the map. "It would keep us hidden from any guards patrolling the wall."

"Okay." Axen stood. "We should get going before it gets too dark to travel."

Our hosts replenished our supplies and sent us on our way. Walking through the woods proved much easier on a full stomach, and we continued with confident steps. Not long after, the trees became scraggly and sparse as we neared the edge of the forest. Up ahead, I could see the end of the woods and the sky, but that was all. We approached what I assumed was the edge of the world. Once there, I saw the earth dropped deep into itself, and a massive crack extended for miles. The green of the forest died away, and all that was left were rocks and dust leading down into the canyon. The ravine loomed bigger than the map had let on.

Axen took the lead down the side of the gorge. "Watch your step."

A rough path had been worn into the ground, leading us down a precarious trail. I slipped here and there as I tried to keep my balance as we descended, the voices complaining the whole way down. Finally, we reached the bottom. The day seemed to have grown warmer, and I regretted not taking the ladies of the camp up on their offer of some fresh clothes.

"Do we follow this the whole way?" I looked at Axen as I spoke.

"Yeah," he said. "Stay close though. Something doesn't feel right." He picked his way carefully over some rocks and kept glancing around at the rock walls around us.

"Why? I thought we took this way because it was safer?" I could sense nothing wrong.

"Safer from guards, yes. But something is down here. Listen."

We stopped moving, and sure enough, I could hear a low hissing coming from the ravine walls.

"What is it?" I whispered.

"If I knew, I would've told you. Just be careful."

Axen kept walking, and I kept one ear trained on the hiss as we moved along the rock bed. Something seemed strange about the even sound—not an animal's voice, but rather something like gas leaking from a pipe.

I was about to voice my opinion when something caught my eye. A scream erupted from my lips instead. I tried to look away, but couldn't stop staring at the human skeleton, burnt to a crisp, laying against the ravine edge.

"What is it?" Axen came closer as I lifted a shaking finger to point out what I wished I could ignore. He walked over and knelt next to the deceased. "He's been dead for a while now. Clearly, he was burnt to death."

He used a stick to prod at the ground around the human before reaching down and grabbing the remains of a small leather sack hidden beneath the bones. The pouch looked damaged by the burns but had remained somewhat intact. The other contents hadn't been so lucky. Only a few pieces of paper remained among a pile of ash. Axen reached inside and pulled out a singed piece of parchment.

"Can you make out what it is?" I knelt next to him, trying to ignore the stench of burnt flesh.

"I think this piece might say something." Axen wiped off a small fragment of the paper and looked closely. "It says 'She burned.' The rest has been burned off."

"She burned? From what?" I looked around. "Wait. Axen ... how *did* they burn?" I stood and pulled at Axen's shirt. "I think we should keep moving."

Axen stood and started down the ravine again. Every step we took deeper into the cavern caused the hissing to grow louder. Soon, the noise became so deafening I couldn't even hear the voices in my head, let alone Axen. I watched the ground change from stones and dirt to solid black rock the farther we walked. As we neared the middle, I became aware of the temperature rising rapidly. Sweat rolled down my cheeks as I pressed further into the ravine. I started to wheeze. The hazy air wasn't only a result of the heat. Heavy smoke could now be seen in front of us.

"Axen?"

A loud hissing from within the walls masked my voice. The smoke assaulted my lungs as I tried to catch my breath. I tried to turn around, but the walls of the ravine burst into flames, and fire lashed out from within the canyon walls. The impact of the heat knocked me to my knees as I screamed. The flames wrapped around my arm, leaving their marks before continuing down the cavern. I started to crawl, attempting to remain below the mass of smoke. If I didn't find Axen, I'd be lost. I pulled my shirt up over my mouth and nose to filter as much smoke as I could. I stumbled around the flames, searching for where I'd last seen my companion.

Just as I believed I could go no further, I felt a hand grab hold of my shirt and turned to see Axen covering his face with his sleeve. I followed his lead through the inferno. Half crawling our way out of the tunnel of flames, we moved closer to the end of the ravine, leaving the inferno behind us. Climbing up the rock wall, we managed to escape the blazes and rolled onto the grass above. Our lungs rid themselves of the smoke we had ingested. My eyes cleared with each blink and cough as the fresh air destroyed the leftover ash.

I dragged my body close to the edge of the canyon and looked in at the raging fire below. I pulled myself to my feet and walked back to Axen who was dusting the ash from his clothes. Looking at my arm, I saw the bite marks of the flames.

"You're hurt." Axen walked over to inspect the burns and searched our supplies for a bandage. He poured water from our canteen onto the wound. His eyes showed careful consideration of each move as he spread a salve onto my arms. As he wrapped me with bandages, I realized that despite his intense exterior, his touch felt gentle and caring. "That should help."

"Thank you."

I held my arm close to me as we walked away from the ravine. Looking ahead, I could see small huts built from mud. The villagers saw us and rushed out to greet us.

"Are you two all right?" a woman asked.

"We're fine. We got caught in a fire in the ravine."

Axen wiped the sweat from his brow but only succeeded in spreading more soot across his face. I assumed the layers of black dust made us look much worse than we felt.

"We're here from the base camp," I jumped in. "We were sent by Aldred in search of the Final Answer. I never knew it would be this dangerous."

"Please"—the lady ushered us toward the camp—"come inside and rest. You two have been through a lot."

They introduced themselves, and we were led into the home of the woman. Once inside and settled, the woman gave us rags to wash off our faces. She set a platter with steaming rolls, thin slices of meat, and a variety of vegetables on the table.

"Can I do anything to help?" I asked.

"Oh no, dear. You and Axen rest and eat. Now, you were asking about the Final Answer. I don't have it, but my grandmother passed down something I think may be important. Wait one moment." The woman left the room and soon returned with a slip of paper. "It is a quote from a book one of my ancestors wrote. I believe it may mean something when it comes to the Final Answer."

I took the paper from her hand and read it aloud. "'She burned too bright for this world' by Emily Brontë in *Wuthering Heights*." I looked at Axen. *That must have been the same quote the man had before he burned in the ravine.* "Did you, by chance, send a man out from here with that quote?"

"Yes, we did. We sent a scout to go find another camp, and he never returned. Why? Do you know him?"

"I'm sorry to tell you this, ma'am, but we found the scout at the bottom of the ravine. He was not as lucky as we were in escaping the fire." Axen spoke solemnly.

"Oh …" The woman sat down. "He was a dear friend of mine. I had a feeling something had happened."

The remainder of dinner was quiet. Axen and I tried our best to help clean up, but she wouldn't have it. Afterwards, the woman laid out some fresh clothes and made up spots for us to sleep.

Then, she rejoined us at the table. "I suppose you'll be on your way in the morning?"

"Yes," Axen said. "Do you have a map to the next nearest camp?"

"I don't know if it is the next closest, but I do have a map." She pulled a rolled piece of parchment from a shelf while Axen laid our map on the table. The woman unrolled her portion and matched it against ours. "Looks like a perfect match." The newest addition of the map showed a large lake to the west. Slightly above it was the mark of the next camp.

"I'm guessing we can go over this lake to reach the camp?" Axen questioned.

"You could. Or you can go under the lake through tunnels that were built long ago."

"I guess it wouldn't matter either way. But I think we should decide in the morning. Let's get some sleep."

With that, Axen turned in, and the woman went about some evening chores.

I stared at our map and the never-ending world it depicted. *I didn't sign up for this much chaos. Which way will be a calmer trip than today?* I stayed in that spot until my eyes started to drift closed from exhaustion. Finally, I gave in and slept.

***

To go ACROSS THE LAKE, *turn to page 77*
To go UNDER THE LAKE, *turn to page 83*

THROUGH THE FIELD—THE SCARLET LETTER

"I'd rather walk through a field than try to climb in and out of a ravine." I pulled the map toward me but Axen pulled it back just as quick.

"Field it is. We better get moving." Axen folded the map, thanked the men of the camp, and we set out through the woods.

The sun streamed through the trees more in that part of the forest, warming our skin and creating a pleasant moment of peace.

The edge of the field was easy to spot at the end of the woods and the wind rustled through the tall grass that seemed to stretch for miles. As we stepped into the sea of green, the smells of wildflowers and dew attacked my senses. I never knew a scent could make my head spin.

The flowers and stalks of grass extended far above our heads in some areas, making it difficult to tell if we were heading in the right direction. Moving farther into the field, I looked ahead and saw we still had most of the field ahead of us despite walking for quite some time.

"Are we going the right way?" I stole a look at the map. The afternoon sun began its decline, but we had barely started into the field. "Shouldn't we be to the other side by now?"

"We must have underestimated the size." Axen veered to the right and pushed through an extra dense area of greenery. After a few more hours of wandering, I saw a familiar patch of flowers. It seemed we had gone in circles. We were only inches closer to the end than when we'd started. My legs started to feel heavy as we trudged along.

"Axen, is it just me, or does it seem like this field has no end?"

"I'm not sure, but this heat sure isn't helping." Axen wiped the sweat from his forehead, and I tried to shield my eyes. He was right. The sun was beating down on us, and I could feel my skin tightening as it burned. We kept moving, but every step made it feel like I had concrete in my limbs.

"I'm not sure how much farther I can go." I sat down in the grass, my body begging me to rest. "Shouldn't it be getting dark by now? We've been walking for hours."

"Something is strange about this. It should be well past dark, and we should be through the field by now." Axen bent over, put his hands on his knees, and took a few deep breaths.

"This may seem funny, but do you feel like there is extra weight on you?"

"Yes. I felt it after we entered the field. It's almost as if gravity has doubled, pulling us into the ground. We can't stay here." Axen reached out a hand and helped me to stand. "We need to keep moving. Don't stop."

I trudged along behind him. As we neared the center of the field, I noticed that the sun had finally moved a little farther down in the sky. Maybe time was slower here. I looked back at the ground and jumped.

"Ah!" A shadow had caught my eye—something lurking in the tall grass.

"What is it?" Axen joined me.

"I'm not sure. There's something over here."

I pressed the weeds down with my boot and revealed a rather gruesome sight. I screamed and jumped back. A human corpse lay in the grass. Dead for days, the body had started to decay, and bugs crawled their way over the sickly pale skin. An awful smell mixed with the thick scent of the field caused me to gag. I turned away as Axen knelt next to the body.

"There's something here." I heard him rummaging through the grass. Soon, he came up with a small satchel in his hand. "He must have been carrying this."

Axen opened the pouch and pulled out a piece of map, much like the one we had been given at the last camp, as well as a slip of paper that seemed to have had writing on it at one point. The pencil marks were smudged and illegible except for a few words.

"She ... weight ... felt ... freedom." I read aloud the words I could make out. "I wonder if it's another clue to the Final Answer."

"It might be, but we won't know unless we can make it out of here alive." Axen scanned our surroundings. The end of the green sea still seemed forever away. "We need to move quickly. Try to ignore the weight and push through. We have got to get out of here." Axen placed the satchel and its contents in his bag, and we started off as fast as our burdened legs would allow.

Keeping my eyes on the horizon, I heard the voices cheering me on. *Only a little farther. Keep going. Don't stop or you'll die.* They may have been a little harsher than necessary, but they did the trick and I persevered.

An eternity had seemingly passed when I finally saw the end of the field. I dragged my body out of the high grass and fell to the ground. Leaving the field seemed to make time return to its normal pace, and the sun hurried on its descent. The weight lifted off me, and I sighed. Axen laid next to me, his breathing labored.

"And here I thought the field would be the easier of the two treks." I laughed at myself and stood, brushing the dirt from my pants.

Axen pulled the map from his pocket and looked around. "We shouldn't be too far from the camp. I think it's just over this hill."

We set off again and, before long, spotted a small village ahead. I walked a little faster knowing we were so close to the end of this stretch of our adventure. A few people from the camp caught sight of us, and a woman walked down a path to greet us.

"Who are you?" she called.

"We're friends," I responded. "We're from the base camp."

The lady seemed to relax a bit and made her way to us. "Well, hello! You two must be tired to have come all that way. Come. I'll give you a place to rest. What are your names?"

"I'm Calessa, and this is Axen."

The woman led us to a small hut and gave us something to eat. "What brings you all the way from the base camp?"

"We were sent to see if you had found the Final Answer," Axen said between bites.

"I see. I'm afraid that must mean our scout never made it there. We have what we believe is a clue to the Final Answer. I had sent a scout out weeks ago to find another camp to tell them."

My mind flashed an image of the corpse we had seen earlier. "I'm so sorry, but you're right. We came across your scout in a field we traveled through. I'm sorry to say he didn't make it."

"Oh my ..." The woman sat down. "I was afraid he had gotten lost, but I never thought the trip would be dangerous enough for that." Her eyes filled with tears.

"I'm sorry." I teared up watching her.

She stifled a sob and cleared her throat. "Well, there will be plenty of time to grieve. For now, I need to get you that clue." She scurried to another room and returned with a book and a piece of parchment. "Here is the book that has the clue. An original copy of *The Scarlet Letter* by Nathaniel Hawthorne. The author underlined a passage I think may be important." The woman opened the book and handed it to me.

"'She had not known the weight until she felt the freedom.'"

Axen took the book and read to himself as the woman unrolled the parchment she had brought.

"I'm assuming you two will be on your way in the morning, but I wanted to give you this piece of a map I have. I sent a different one with the scout. This one shows the next camp north of here. I believe you can either go through an underground tunnel the leads under this lake or you can choose to go around. That way may take longer but who knows what kind of condition that tunnel is in." She pointed out our options on the parchment, while Axen pulled out our map to line up with the new piece.

"We can decide in the morning," I said. "After that trek through the field of weight, I am beyond tired." I could feel my body starting to shut down as we spoke.

The woman set up a cot for me and a spot on a couch for Axen and left us to drift off. It didn't take long.

***

To go UNDER THE LAKE, *turn to page 83*
To go AROUND THE LAKE, *turn to page 89*

ALONG THE RIVER—PETER PAN

"I vote we stay along the river," Axen said.

"If you think that's best." I wiped the sleepiness from my eyes.

"It makes the most sense. It's safer than mountain ranges and more likely to be easy travel."

"He has a point," the woman piped in as Axen collected our supplies.

"I'm not going to argue the idea of easy walking."

After saying goodbye to the woman and a few other villagers, we set out through the fields next to the village. Climbing over a slight hill, I saw the river in the distance.

As we got close, a cool breeze wafted from the water and brushed against my skin. I could smell the freshness of morning. The sun glinted off the clear water, illuminating the riverbed. The bottom was filled with gem-colored pebbles which created a colorful mosaic and made tiny rainbows dance through the stream.

"Axen, isn't it beautiful?"

"I guess."

"Oh, come on. Even a grumpy fugitive should be able to acknowledge beauty once in a while." I jabbed a playful fist at Axen's shoulder, and he stopped.

Without turning around, he spoke in an even tone. "If you knew half of what I've seen, you'd know the world is never as beautiful as it seems."

The lightheartedness of the moment vanished. "What happened to you back at Answers Headquarters?"

"You don't want to know." He kept his eyes focused forward.

"But I do. I mean, you told me once that you were still 'infected'? What does that mean?" I pulled him around to face me.

"Just forget it." His eyes flickered.

"I want to know what happened."

"Forget it." He spoke the words through gritted teeth.

"Look—"

Axen turned away and started walking. Pressing the issue would only cause trouble. I put my hands up in surrender and fell once again in step beside him.

After a few steps, I glanced up and noticed the sun was already on its way down, though it felt as if we had only been walking for an hour at most.

"Axen, is it as late as I think it is? The sun is already going down."

"What?" Axen looked up. "It doesn't feel like we've been walking that long."

"Maybe we aren't keeping track. Let's keep moving."

We walked a while longer and dusk fell. We picked a spot along the river and made a fire before getting out some dinner.

"This has to be the quickest day I've ever experienced." I spoke between bites. "I'm not even tired for having walked for at least eight hours. It only felt like two."

"We should still try to get some rest." Axen finished his meal, and we made ourselves comfortable for the night.

I felt as if I had just dozed off when the morning sun burst over the horizon. I squinted in the bright light and pulled myself to my feet. After shaking Axen awake, I packed our things and we continued along the river.

FAITH WEAVER

I kept a close eye on the sun as we walked. It traveled across the sky in what appeared to be record time, and before we knew it, the moon was rising yet again. Sitting around another campfire, only a few miles from the last one, my mind tried to grasp what was happening.

"Time must move quicker in this realm."

"It appears so. I guess we can keep traveling through the night if you'd like."

I shrugged. "We might as well. We've already been away from the camp two days. We were supposed to be at the next camp yesterday."

We put out our fire and walked under the stars, trying to reach the end of our path before losing too many more days. A few hours ... or days ... passed, and we spent most of them traveling along the stream. We stopped occasionally to eat and rest but kept a steady pace.

After a few hours, or days, in this realm, I saw a bend in the river and a path leading away from it. Following the trail led us over a hill and straight to the gates of a small city in a valley. Brick buildings lined cobblestone streets. People bustled about and dozens of different conversations hit my ears. A guard sauntered over to the gate, a glint of sunlight shining off the sword attached to the belt on his hip.

"Who are you?" The man's broad shoulders and rough facial hair matched his gruff voice.

"I'm Axen, and this is Calessa."

"What brings you to the city?" the man asked.

"We were sent by Aldred, to see if you have the Final Answer," Axen replied.

"You're from the base camp?"

I joined the conversation. "Technically, we're from Ashkelan, but we escaped and found the base camp. Aldred sent us off from there."

"I see. Well, come in. Darzon will want to meet you." The guard returned to his post and pulled a lever. The gate swung open with a screech on rusty hinges.

The guard closed the gate—complete with more screeching—and led us through the city. Mist from the small fountain at the center of town splashed against my arm. People chattered as they stole glances at us, mistrust glimmering in their eyes. The city reminded me of Ashkelan, and while it was familiar, brought little comfort now that I had seen the world outside.

We reached a large, stone building, and the guard knocked on the ornately carved wooden door. A man answered. Ducking to step through the doorway, he dwarfed the guard both in size and intimidating demeanor.

"Hello! And who do we have here?"

"Darzon, sir, these are travelers from the base camp. They have come about the Final Answer."

"Wonderful! Come in!"

Unlike the guard, Darzon's appearance conflicted with his friendly tone. He ushered us inside with a smile and sent the guard back to the gate.

Darzon's home was much larger than anything I had seen outside Ashkelan and felt luxurious compared to the past few camps we had visited. Darzon offered us a drink, and we gathered around a table. My eyes flitted to the grand settees, vaulted ceilings, and bright artwork covering the pristine walls.

"If you are here for the complete Final Answer, I don't have it," Darzon began. I shut my gaping mouth and turned to face our host. "I do however know that it has something to do with the quotes of our ancestors. Most of us readers outside Ashkelan are descendants of one author or another, and I believe those authors have hidden clues to the Final Answer within the texts of their works, knowing only readers would be able to find them." Darzon stood and went into another room, returning with an antique box. Opening it, he pulled out a well-worn book. "An ancestor of one of the readers who lived here wrote this book called *Peter Pan*. Inside, he underlined a specific phrase. Here, read it for yourselves."

I slid the book across the table and read the quote aloud. "'I suppose it's like the ticking crocodile, isn't it? Time is chasing after all of us.'" I looked up at Axen. "It's like the faster time along the river. Have you noticed all the clues we have gotten seem to relate to something that's happened? How did the authors know?"

"Ah," Darzon chimed in. "I don't believe that is by chance alone. I remember the ancestor of J.M. Barrie, the man who wrote *Peter Pan*, used to say it was known in her family that the ones who were destined to know the Final Answer would find their way through these quotes." Darzon pulled the book back to him. "We also believe the secret to these quotes lies in the first letter. You can see here the author made an extra mark under the 'I' in the sentence."

"So, the quotes, or rather the letters that start them, are somehow connected to the Final Answer?" The voices started rambling in my head, trying to make the connection.

"I believe so, yes." Darzon put the book back in the box and pulled out a piece of parchment. "I have a section of a map here. It may be useful on your journey."

Axen pulled out our map and placed it next to the piece Darzon had spread on the table. Our world expanded once more. A marshy area covered the west, and a new forest appeared to the north. A camp was marked above the two with two faint paths leading to it.

"I'm guessing our options are either to go through this swamp here or through that forest?" I pointed out the sketched trails on the map.

"Yes, though I'm sorry I can't tell you which is the faster path. I would recommend getting some rest before you head off on your way though. The trek will take you the better part of a day, and I wouldn't want you traveling at night."

Darzon set us up for the night, and Axen and I both took his offer of some dinner before we crashed. As I drifted off, the voices spoke in whispers. *I wonder if I am the descendent of an author. Is that why I can read? I wonder what the letters stand for. Maybe they spell ...*

***

To go THROUGH THE SWAMP, *turn to page 95*
To go THROUGH THE FOREST, *turn to page 101*

THROUGH THE MOUNTAIN RANGE—
THE HOBBIT

"The mountain range will give us more security." Axen shoveled bites of breakfast into his mouth between sentences. "We should get an early start. I have a feeling today is going to be a long one."

I finished my food and packed as Axen studied the map before tucking it away in his jacket. A few minutes later, I followed Axen out of the camp, and we headed toward the mountains we saw in the distance. As we neared, I saw a path that led straight into the heart of a stone maze.

"Does the map show how to make it through the pass?" I asked.

"Sort of." Axen squinted at the map. "It looks like it's a pretty straight shot, but then again, this isn't very detailed."

"I guess we keep moving then."

As we neared the entrance to the path, a chill spiraled through me. The shadows started to dance as the sun disappeared behind the mountains. We pressed on without another choice. My skin felt damp as a fog rolled through the passageway. The light breeze of the morning turned cold.

How could the environment change in such a short time? The voice within me spoke with reason for once. I turned to see Axen mumbling under his breath. We both seemed to know something dangerous awaited us, and I had a bad feeling we were about to find out what it was. The wind grew aggressive and lashed out at my hair and clothes. I shielded my eyes and pressed forward.

Hearing a shout to my left, I looked in time to see our map ripped from Axen's hands, the wind carrying it down the passageway and out of sight. Breaking into a run, we rounded the corner but soon stopped in our tracks. A wide expanse amid the mountains stretched before us, every inch covered by bits of parchment. The wind rushed through the center, creating a whirlwind of paper. The edges of the cave were filled with stacks and piles of the mysterious documents.

"What is this place?" I wandered over to a pile and lifted the top sheet. "It's a map."

"They all are." Axen began sorting through a heap of scattered sheets on the other side.

"But why are they here? How did they all get here?" I crept farther into the cavern, staying close to the edge to avoid the paper tornado.

"I'm not sure, but last time I checked, only one creature is known to hoard their favorite things like this." Axen looked at me, and his blue eyes lit up with fear. "Don't. Move."

"Why?"

Axen held a finger to his lips. I took a step forward but then froze. The cold air had turned hot. Gusts of warm air hit my back as if the mountain breathed. Axen motioned for me to inch toward him. Careful not to step on the mounds of crumpled paper, I reached Axen and turned to see what sort of beast the mountains had become. But it wasn't the mountain at all.

"What is that thing?" I whispered.

"A dragon."

The giant creature lay amidst the parchment sleeping soundly. Its body looked like parchment itself, with etchings of the realms scattered across it like scars. Its wings were folded behind as it lay curled in what appeared to be a nest of maps in an alcove off the side of the cavern. Bits of paper had been torn and stuck at varying angles to create a mane around its large head. Without a careful eye, no one would even see the creature camouflaged against its surroundings.

"Is it dangerous?" I whispered.

"They can be." Axen began inching toward the other end of the cave. "They are peaceful creatures but don't take kindly to humans taking their treasure. However, without our map, we have no direction. Our best bet is to find ours and get out without waking her."

"How can you tell it's a girl?"

"Only females tend to hoard things, while male dragons are the more aggressive type." Axen began rustling through stacks of maps, and I joined him on the search for ours, looking over at the dragon every few moments to assure myself she wasn't creeping up on us. Nearing the other end of the cavern, I turned to the whirlwind of parchment and noticed a familiar piece.

"Axen, look!" I pointed at the spiral. "Our map is in there. I can see the pieces stuck together. There it is again!" I watched as our map was tossed in circles as the wind swirled. I stepped closer, hoping to snatch it as the mini tornado came around. I kept my eyes focused but a loud thump to my right sent a shiver up my spine. I turned to see our sleeping beauty had awoken, and she didn't look happy.

The dragon stood over twice my height. While terrifying, she was a beautiful creature too. Her wings look like charred maps extending from her back and spread wide as if she was about to charge. She snorted and her front talons swiped out at me. I jumped to avoid the attack. Stumbling, I ended up in the middle of the tornado, the wind whipping the parchment around me as I tried to see through. I saw our map fly past and grabbed at it. Tiny cuts laced my body as the wind made the parchment fight back. I snagged our map and shoved it quickly in my jacket. I turned and saw that the dragon had moved between me and the exit, where Axen waited with wide eyes.

Run! The voice screamed, and I did. I burst through the edge of the tornado and rolled under the dragon's belly. I grabbed Axen by his jacket and rushed for the exit of the cave as the dragon reared itself around and charged. As we made it to the smaller part of the tunnel, I glanced behind to see the dragon hot on our tail. I kept moving and only stopped when I heard the scraping talons and the angry growls from the beast start to fade. The giant beast couldn't make it into this part of the tunnel.

"That was close."

"Too close." Axen panted next to me.

I was about to sigh in relief until I saw the dragon back up into her lair and look up. I followed her gaze and knew what she was thinking. I looked back in time to see her take off, soaring into the sky.

"She's going to try to beat us to the edge of the mountains!" I took off running, praying Axen would follow. I jetted down the path—thankfully a straight shot to the end of the range. Emerging into the sun, I scanned the clouds but saw nothing.

"The camp's over there." Axen pointed. "If we move quickly, we can make it before she finds us."

We hurried toward the large wall that appeared to be securing a small city within. I saw a guard standing watch. He must have seen us coming as he had the main gate unlocked before we even reached it. Ushering us inside, he shut the iron bars behind us and turned. His hand rested on the hilt of his sword.

"Who are you?" he asked.

I made introductions and filled him in on our adventure so far, checking over my shoulder every few seconds. The guard must have noticed my anxious looks.

"Don't worry about the dragon," he stated. "She never comes this far. She knows our weapons are stronger than her paper wings. Darzon, the leader of this city will want to meet you. Follow me."

Walking through this city made me feel like I was back in Ashkelan. Its stone walls, massive buildings, and town square were distinct from the more rural camps we had seen so far.

The guard led us to a home and knocked on the door. A burly man answered and beamed at us.

"Hello! And who do we have here?"

"Hello, Darzon." The guard tipped his head in regards. "This is Axen and Calessa. They are here about the Final Answer. Aldred sent them." The guard then turned and walked away without further statement.

Darzon motioned for us to come inside. "I was hoping you would show up."

"You knew we were coming?" I asked.

"Well, not you two exactly, but I knew one day someone would come searching. Here, have a seat."

I took in the grand setting. His house was the size of four of the homes I was used to seeing in Ashkelan. Oversized seats and glass-topped tables filled the area. Darzon left for a moment, only to return quickly with a book in hand.

"Here. The next clue to your journey." Darzon handed us the book: *The Hobbit* by J. R. R. Tolkien. I opened it to a marked page.

"'It does not do to leave a live dragon out of your calculations if you live near him.'" I looked up in surprise and opened my mouth.

Darzon raised his hand to quiet my question. "It has been known in this city for many generations that one day an adventurer would come searching for the Final Answer and find their way only through these quotes. Am I right to believe you had an encounter with a dragon?"

I nodded.

"Ah, I thought so. I wish I could tell you more, but the only other piece of the answer I have is that you will find the solution within these quotes. I believe it may have something to do with the first letter. In this copy, the initial 'I' in the sentence has been marked under. I believe it is of some significance. But now, I think you two are probably in need of some food."

As we ate, Darzon gave us a piece of a map to add on to our existing one. "I don't think you should start your travels again until daybreak. You can stay here for the night. The next camp is a good journey away, and neither possible route is safe in the dark. You can either go this way through the forest, or you can take a shortcut over this river here." Darzon gave little in the way of advice on which to take, and, instead, left Axen and I to mull over the decision while he set up cots for us.

That night as I tried to sleep, the voices spoke in whispers. *What do the first letters have to do with it? Why would a single letter matter when we need a whole sentence? I wonder ...*

***

To go THROUGH THE FOREST, *turn to page 101*
To go OVER THE RIVER, *turn to page 107*

ACROSS THE LAKE—LITTLE WOMEN

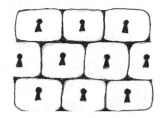

"Going across the lake would give a more direct line of sight, I think." Axen packed our things as he spoke.

"Yes, but unless you're hiding a boat somewhere, how are we going to get across?" I finished my breakfast and went to help my companion.

"There's been tales that everything you need to cross will be found at the lake."

Axen and I turned to the woman.

"So, we're meant to go with no supplies or plan?" I asked, eyebrows raised.

"Yes," she said. "You shouldn't have a need for anything out of the ordinary on this leg of your trip."

"Well then, I guess we're all set." Axen swung his pack onto his shoulders and we thanked our host and left.

The cool air brought a light rain to start our day, and the dreary skies made it easy to fall into a gloomy state of mind. Ambling on, I sidled up to Axen, hoping to stay a bit warmer in his presence. I glanced at the map and saw that the lake should be on the other side of the small hill up ahead.

"Do you think it will take the whole day to get to the next camp?"

Axen grunted. "I sure hope not, but with our luck, probably."

I huddled a little closer as we walked and looked up to see Axen staring straight ahead. The rain stuck to his eyelashes, and his dark hair blew across his forehead. His ice-colored eyes focused. *He's handsome in a roguish kind of way.* My cheeks warmed at the voices' opinion, and I willed them to behave themselves. Now was not the time for feelings to pop up.

Reaching the top of the hill, I breathed the misty air to clear my head and looked down at the lake ahead of us. Or at least, what I assumed was the lake. A massive cloud of fog covered a wide expanse. My boots sunk deeper into the marshy earth. We were definitely near water.

The fog thickened as we drew closer, and I tried to focus my vision. My boot hit something hard, causing me to trip forward. Axen's arm snaked around my middle and pulled me close to him to keep me from falling.

"You okay?" he asked.

I looked up and was caught off guard at how close his face was to mine. "I-uh-y-yes. I'm okay."

I struggled to regain composure as I found my footing. I nudged where I had tripped with my boot and found the hard surface that caused this embarrassing moment: the edge of a dock. When I carefully stepped up on the platform, the fog dissipated to the sides.

"Look, there." Axen pointed ahead of us. "There's a stand at the end of the dock."

I walked to the stand and saw three items.

"A key, a feather, and a piece of paper? How is this supposed to help us across a lake we can't even see?" I picked up the items and opened the folded parchment. "'Trust the clouds,'" I read. "What's that supposed to mean?" Axen looked over my shoulder as the fog began to shift, rolling to the sides, revealing a path out onto the lake.

FAITH WEAVER

I tested the cloud walkway with my foot—soft, but somehow secure. Holding my breath, I stepped off the dock and felt the fog move beneath my feet. I could tell I was standing over water and looked back to see an apprehensive Axen. I grabbed his hand, pulling him off the dock.

"Hey!" he exclaimed as he stumbled off the edge.

"You're fine." I snickered and pulled him along as we started across the lake.

Soon, he let go of my hand, and the voices protested. *It felt safer with my hand in his.* I let out a small gasp when I realized the voices no longer spoke to me, but from me. *Can I control this? Wait. I am controlling this. This is me. I'm the voice!*

My trail of words was interrupted when I bumped into Axen. Looking up, I saw what had made him stop. Ahead loomed a huge wall. It stood taller than the fog allowed us to see and wider than the path allowed by the clouds. The stones had an odd texture about them as if something was stuck to the middle of each piece.

"What's in the center of the rocks?" I asked.

"I don't know." Axen walked closer, then looked back at me. "Bring me that key from the dock."

Confused, I pulled the key from my pocket and walked toward Axen. As I neared, I knew why he had asked. The center of every stone held a keyhole. I handed the key to Axen. He placed it in the first one he reached, but the key wouldn't turn. He tried again with no luck. I let my eyes scan the wall and lost count of the amount of stones. There had to be at least four hundred squares and still more beyond the fog.

"How do we know which one it is? This could take days to figure out. And what about the ones we can't reach?" My breath quickened. The last time I had been locked inside a wall, the entire world was outside. I felt myself start to panic and looked to Axen for strength. He didn't seem too interested in my dilemma, though, as he continued to try each lock and worked his way toward the center of the wall.

I forced my breathing to slow on my own and started to scan the wall for anything that might prove different from the rest. After several minutes of searching, I spotted a stone near the bottom that was inlaid a little deeper than the others. Kneeling on the shaky path, I called to Axen.

"Come look at this. I think I found it." Axen came to my side, and we looked closer. "This keyhole is round."

Axen held up the key to the hole. There was no way it would fit. "Guess that's not the right one after all." He started to stand to go back to his search.

The feather.

"Wait! What if the key isn't what you need to unlock the wall?"

I pulled the feather from my jacket and stuck the spindled end into the circular lock. I heard a click as I turned. I jumped back as a portion of the wall tipped up to reveal a doorway. Through the frame, a large room appeared. The floors sparkled like diamonds, and the ceiling was lost in the clouds above. My jaw dropped as I stepped into the massive space.

"What is this place?" I wondered aloud.

"I'm not sure, but I don't recommend staying to find out." Axen sauntered across the great room to a door on the opposite side. I took my time and marveled at this palace as I made my way to the other side. Reaching Axen, I watched as he opened the door to show another cloudy pathway. Glancing over my shoulder one last time, I followed him out and we continued on our way.

Not too long after, we saw the edge of the lake. Stepping off the fog onto solid ground, I looked to see a great walled city in the valley ahead. We made our way to the gate, where a young guard greeted us.

"Who are you, and why have you come here?"

"We're travelers from the base camp. Aldred has sent us to find the Final Answer," Axen stated.

The guard opened the gate wide and ushered us in. "Well, in that case, please, come in! Darzon will be happy to meet you."

The guard led us through the city to the home of whom I could only assume was their leader. A great stone mansion stood at the edge of town. Reaching the wooden door, my eyes flitted over the intricate carvings as the guard stepped up and knocked. A middle-aged man answered. His gruff look contradicted his smiling eyes as he greeted us.

"Well, hello! Who do we have here?"

Introductions were made, and soon Axen and I were being ushered inside for some dinner and conversation. Soon after, Darzon brought a book from another room and handed it to me.

"*Little Women* by Louisa May Alcott." I turned to a marked page and read the quote. "'I've got the key to my castle in the air, but whether I can unlock the door remains to be seen.'" I traced my finger over the words. Glancing at Darzon, I questioned, "Why is the first letter emphasized?"

"Ah, you see, our ancestors believed that the Final Answer will be revealed through these quotes. Specifically, the first letters. They say whoever is destined to learn the answer must live these quotes through their journey to the truth."

Axen and I glanced at each other knowingly. It appeared we were in this for the long haul.

"Do you, by chance, have a map to the next nearest camp?" Axen asked.

"Yes, there in the book is a piece of a map that I had stored for a moment like this. You will find two paths you could take. There is a sparse forest to the east of the camp and a jungle to the right."

"I think we should decide in the morning." I spoke through a yawn.

The men agreed, and our host graciously made up some cots. I wandered over to Axen who was mulling over the map and put my hand on his shoulder. I could feel his muscles tense a bit at my touch.

"Goodnight, Axen. I'll see you in the morning." I pulled my hand away and started to head toward my makeshift bed.

Axen turned around and looked at me, his eyes soft. "G-goodnight, Calessa, sleep well." He returned to his map.

My mind raced as I lie in bed, replaying the moment in his arms earlier that day. *Maybe I'm not crazy to have feelings like this. Maybe he has them too.*

***

If you've been through the Fiery Ravine, GO THROUGH THE SPARSE WOODS by *turning to page 113*.

If you've met the mysterious creature in the woods, GO THROUGH THE JUNGLE by *turning to page 119*.

UNDER THE LAKE—JOURNEY TO THE CENTER OF THE EARTH

"Considering we don't have a boat, I guess going under the lake would be our best option." Axen sat at the table studying our growing map.

"Be careful in that underground tunnel." The woman started to pack our things as she spoke. "I've heard it can be dangerous."

"We'll be careful," I said, grabbing my jacket.

Soon, we were on our way. The cool morning woke my tired body and gave me a fresh feeling to start the day's journey. Wandering along, I heard the voices start to ramble. *I wonder if we'll ever find the answer. I hope we do. Otherwise I'm traveling alone with a fugitive for nothing.* I smirked to myself then stilled. *Wait. This voice. It's not someone in my head, it's me. I'm controlling it.*

Axen looked at me and raised an eyebrow. "You all right?"

"Uh, yes. I think so." I shook my head to clear it. "You said you got used to the voices. Can you control yours too?"

"Yes. The voices are your inner thoughts. Whatever you think or dream or imagine comes from that voice." Axen kept his eyes straight ahead as he spoke.

Before I could say more, I spotted the lake up ahead. Fog covered the entire area, leaving no trace of the water beneath.

The closer we walked, the heavier the fog became, masking our path. I could barely make out a small dock. Stepping up to it, I looked at the edge. Something seemed strange about some of the planks. I reached down and noticed a small area that had been worn down. Pressing my fingers to it, I heard a click, and the floorboards of the dock shifted to reveal a set of stairs leading beneath the lake.

"Do you still have that torch we packed?"

I turned to see that Axen had already retrieved it from our pack. Letting him pass, I followed him down into the tunnel. The stairs squeaked but seemed sturdy enough and soon the path leveled out. The wooden floors stretched as far as I could see in the dim light of the torch.

"Do you hear that?" Axen's tone was hushed. "It sounds like metal scraping in the walls."

I heard it too. Placing my hand against the wooden siding, I could feel a faint pulse of something moving behind it. Axen took a step deeper into the tunnel but jumped back when a loud crash sounded.

Metal pendulums sliced through the walls, the closest one barely missing Axen as it swung. A scream escaped my lips as I stumbled back.

"Well, this makes things more difficult," Axen growled.

"How are we supposed to get past them?" I eyed the five blades swinging across our path.

"Wait." Axen concentrated on the blades. "They're moving in a rhythm. If we can find an opening, we can make a run for it."

"Yeah, and if we miss the opening, we'll be sliced to bits. Great plan."

"You have any better ideas? We have to get through somehow and that lake up there looked just as dangerous."

I sighed. "Fine. But if we die, I'm blaming you." Ripping a strand of leather from my fraying jacket, I pulled my hair from my face and tied it, then stepped up beside Axen. Watching the pendulums carefully, I started to see the rhythm he was talking about. If we timed it right, we could make it through.

"On my count," Axen said. "Ready … go!" We took off as the first blade passed. Running straight, we managed to clear three of the five. I glanced to my left and saw the fourth heading my way and froze. I could feel the rush of air as the metal razors sliced past me.

"Calessa! You have to keep going! Find your opening and go," Axen shouted from the other side of the contraption.

You can do this. Find the opening. There it was. Wait … ready … go! I ran through the final two spaces and collapsed to the floor. As I began to sit up, I noticed the floor had evenly spaced holes lined from wall to wall. I listened and could hear the metallic sound from the walls coming now from underneath.

"Axen, back up!" I pushed myself backward before metal spikes shot up from the floor. My breathing heavy, I stood and walked to Axen. The spikes lowered back into the floor and exchanged places with ones that sprung down from the ceiling ahead. Another mechanism to navigate.

This time, I quickly noticed the pattern, and Axen and I stepped up to prepare. Counting down, we sprinted forward on one, the sharp sound of the spikes behind us. After we'd made it through, I checked for other dangers. Finding no immediate ones, I took a deep breath and looked ahead to our exit.

"There's the stairs out." I pointed.

"Yeah, but I guarantee there's going to be at least one more surprise before we get there."

Before I had a chance to think of a response, I heard a roar from within the walls. The noise rose to a deafening level and I turned to Axen.

"What is that?" I shouted.

"It sounds like water. The lake must be deeper here and is pressing into the walls. We need to move before it collapses the tunnel," Axen yelled.

I turned to run for the exit and, as I did, felt the floor shift beneath me. I looked down to see that the panels under my feet were sliding into the walls, leaving a huge hole into a deep pit below.

"Run!" I took off, hoping Axen had heard my warning. The floor seemed to disappear as I ran. Taking a leap from the last bit of solid floor—my time was almost up—I landed hard against the stairs. My ribs smashed against the harsh edges. Axen landed next to me a moment later, and we both scrambled up the steps and out a trap door into the sun. Collapsing to the ground, I gasped for air as my ribcage shuttered with pain.

Axen knelt by my side as I wheezed. "Are you okay?"

"I think I may have bruised something, but I'll be okay." I tried to force a smile but only managed a grimace as I tried to stand. Axen put his arm around me and hoisted me up, letting me use him as support.

"The camp's up ahead. Let me help you."

Looking through blurred vision, I could just make out a walled city in a valley not too far away. I was about to thank Axen when everything went black.

***

The soft cushions I woke on made me want to slip back into unconsciousness, but I forced my eyes to focus. Rich colored furniture and a grand staircase proved that the soft settee I was on wasn't the only luxury in this home. I sat up with a wince of pain and looked around. Across the room, Axen sat at a table with a man. They spoke in hushed tones but soon realized I was awake.

"Calessa, this is Darzon," Axen called from his seat. "He's the leader of this town and has been gracious enough to open his home to us for the night."

"Thank you," I said quietly.

"My pleasure," Darzon said. "I hope you're feeling better."

"I am, thank you. Still a little sore, but much better." I turned to Axen. "Did you ask him about the Final Answer?"

"Yes, he said he has another quote for us. He wanted to wait until you were awake to give it to us."

"Can we see it now?"

Darzon chuckled. "Yes, give me a moment." He walked away and returned with a book and what I could only assume was a piece of a map. Handing the book to us, I looked at the cover. *Journey to the Center of the Earth* by Jules Verne.

I opened to a marked page and read the quote aloud. "'If at every instant we may perish, so at every instant we may be saved.'" I looked at Axen. "How is it that every quote we've found so far has somehow connected to these awful experiences we've been having?"

"Ah," Darzon spoke up. "It has been said that the ones who will find the Final Answer will only reach their goal by following these quotes and living them out. I can only imagine what kind of trouble you both have gone through on this journey."

"Trust us, you don't want to know." Axen took the book and studied the quote. "The first letter has a special marking under it. Do you have any idea why?"

"Well, yes and no. I believe the first letter of each quote is going to spell something. Maybe a bit of the Final Answer. But I'm not sure what it all means yet. Seeing as you two are well on your way, I thought a map to the next camp might be helpful." He unfolded the piece of parchment he had been holding. "You can go through this mountain pass or you can climb up and over the mountain this way. The pass is probably safer, but the climb is a straight shot and could save about a half day of travel. But I don't recommend making that decision until the morning. Get some rest." He handed the map to Axen and then left, and we settled in for the night.

My internal voice stayed strangely quiet after such a long day, and it didn't take long for my body to surrender to the much-needed rest.

***

To go THROUGH THE MOUNTAIN PASS, *turn to page 125.*
To go OVER THE MOUNTAIN, *turn to page 131.*

AROUND THE LAKE—ALICE'S ADVENTURES IN WONDERLAND

For the first time on this trip, Axen and I were not on the same page.

"I think I'd rather stay above ground," I said.

"But going under the lake could keep us concealed."

"But how do we know the tunnel is safe? Once we're down there, there's no knowing what we may find. If it's anything like the last few days, we could die down there. I think we should stay where it's safer." I kept my voice level while the voices yelled in my mind. *I can't believe he wants to risk our lives again! Traveling with a fugitive was a bad idea. He's reckless. He's—*

"Fine. We'll go around." Axen growled as he snatched the map off the table and packed our things.

Well, that was easier than expected. I grabbed my jacket and soon we were on our way, having thanked the woman for all she did. We headed out of the village toward a small hill in the distance. Axen's icy eyes and set jaw told me he was in no mood for conversation, so we traveled in silence.

I let the voices wonder as we walked. *I wonder what the voices in his head sound like. Are they the same as mine? Maybe I'll ask him later when he's not being such a grump.*

A small gasp came from within. *Wait. Am I controlling the voices? No. There's only one voice now. Wait. It's me.*

I caught up to Axen's long strides and asked, "Is the voice in your head able to be controlled?"

He glanced at me with those icy eyes—I'd forgotten about his bad mood.

"Yes. They're your thoughts. Anything you think, know, or could even imagine, can be said in your mind. That's why the scientists who created the Answers were so scared of readers. They didn't like that they didn't know what was going on in their heads."

"So, the voice is just me? All this time, I've been talking to myself?" The idea sounded stranger as I said it.

"Essentially, yes. Though your thoughts can surprise you at times. Sometimes, you think something before you understand why." Axen turned and looked at me. "Your thoughts have power. Use it wisely."

"What kind of power?"

Axen didn't answer and pointed ahead of us instead. "There's the lake."

I looked down the hill but only saw a huge mass of fog. The expanse of mist had to be the place we had been looking for.

"Wow, no wonder the map doesn't suggest crossing the lake. You wouldn't be able to see anything." We headed down the hill but stuck to the edges of the lake.

"Don't get too close. I don't feel like rescuing you today."

Axen took the lead, and I glared at the back of his head. *How stupid does he think I am?*

The brisk air wafting off the lake cooled my steaming mind as we walked. After a while, I noticed we had drifted farther away from the lake. Following the contour of the fog had pushed us away from the edge of the water.

"Axen, I think we're getting off track."

"We have to stay out of the fog."

FAITH WEAVER

We continued, but I could feel the cold fingers of the mist reaching out. My clothes clung to me in the damp air, and my eyes tried to adjust to the growing haze.

"Get farther out," Axen called.

"I don't think we have a choice." I looked around as the fog enveloped us, making my eyes play tricks. "Axen, where are you? I can't see."

"Just keep moving forward. We wouldn't be in this mess if you had listened to me. We could be in a straight tunnel instead of in this chaos."

"Now is not the time to start an argument. Keep talking so I can follow your voice."

"Keep walking, I'm sure we'll be out of the fog soon."

A moment later, I heard a yell followed by a splash.

"Axen?" I called out but got no response. "Axen!" Still nothing. Oh, no. He must have fallen in. How are you going to get him out when you can't even see the water? Think, Calessa, think. The fog has been growing wider, so the water should be to my left. As my voice spoke, I noticed the fog shifting to reveal a path. I followed but as soon as my inner monologue stopped, the smoke filled in the trail, abandoning me in the cloud. Keep thinking! The path cleared.

My mind spoke as I moved, telling myself where the path would lead. Finally, I saw the edge of the lake and then a shadow of Axen's body as he struggled to reach the surface. I dove in, put my arm around Axen's middle, and swam back to shore where I pulled Axen up to the bank. Coughing, I looked around to see we were back in the thick of the fog.

"Are you all right?" I asked.

Axen coughed up water and wiped his mouth on his sleeve. "I think so." He looked flushed from either adrenaline or embarrassment. "Thank you," he said sheepishly. "How did you find where I fell?"

"You know how you said my thoughts have power? Well, I think I figured out one of them." I pictured the path once again, and the fog dissipated to reveal it.

Axen's eyes grew big. "You did that with your mind? How?"

"I'm not sure. If I think about the map and the path that was drawn there, I can almost see it in my mind. Next thing I know, the fog clears."

"Interesting. Do you think you can get us around the lake?"

"I sure hope so." I let my mind focus in on the path again and it reappeared.

With the fog cleared, Axen and I made quick work of the rest of the journey. At the edge of the fog, I rushed to the end of the path. Fresh air hit my lungs and I sighed in relief.

I think I like the outside world. Dangers and all. I looked around and soon saw a large, walled city down in a valley ahead. All sense of calm left my body, and I felt the blood drain from my face.

"Hey, are you alright?" Axen stepped up beside me and followed my gaze to the city.

"It looks like Ashkelan."

"Is that a bad thing? I thought you'd be missing home by now. Didn't you have a family back there?"

My jaw tightened. "Yes, I had a family. But I certainly don't care to go back to them." My voice quivered as I spoke. "Well, except my baby sister. I will have to go back for her." I blinked back a tear. "She would love it out here. She always did take after Mom and me with her sense of adventure. I wish Mom were still around to see the outside." I sniffed and then pushed the emotions back down deep where I thought I'd left them.

"I'm sorry, Calessa." Axen placed a hand on my shoulder.

I breathed deep and started down the valley. We needed to keep going.

Reaching the gate of the city, a young guard came to meet us.

"Welcome! You two don't look too threatening." He smiled.

"Uh, no," Axen said. "We're not threats. We're from the base camp. Aldred sent us. Do you know anything about the Final Answer?"

"Ah!" The guard opened the gate and led us inside.

"Darzon, our leader, has the information you came for. Follow me."

The guard started through the heart of the city, leaving us to trail behind. While the buildings seemed as strong and big as Ashkelan, there was a comforting feel to this town—quite opposite the feeling of being trapped I'd always had.

Reaching a grand door of a mansion, the guard knocked. A man who looked to be twice our age opened it.

"Hello. What brings you to this end of town?" the man asked, eyeing us cautiously.

"Darzon, this is Calessa and Axen. They came about the Final Answer. I thought maybe you would show them what we know."

"Of course! Come in, come in!" Darzon welcomed us into his home and offered us something to drink. "I'm sure you two have had a long journey, so let me cut straight to the point." He grabbed a book from a shelf and sat across from us. "Our ancestors have said the one who is destined to find the Final Answer must do so through these quotes they have left behind. Somehow, the first letter is the most important part, but other than that, I'm afraid I don't know much." He pushed the book across the table. "This is my family's copy of *Alice's Adventures in Wonderland* by Lewis Carroll. Have a look."

I opened the book to a marked page and read the quote. "'It's no use going back to yesterday, because I was a different person then.'"

"If it was my guess," Darzon spoke with kindness, "you two have been through a lot these past few days, and I'm more than willing to bet you feel different from when you began."

"It's true," I said. "I guess we're in this 'til the end."

Axen puffed out a breath. "No use sitting here talking about it. Darzon, do you have a map to the next nearest camp?"

"Yes, here." Darzon pulled some parchment from a box nearby. "There are two ways to get there. You can either go over this mountain or through the desert to the west. But I would caution against leaving now. You can stay here tonight."

We agreed, and Darzon set up some cots for us. Lying down, I let my mind drift back to the fog. *If I had told myself yesterday that I would be controlling things with my mind, I would've thought I was crazy. Not that I'm convinced I'm not.*

***

To go OVER THE MOUNTAIN, *turn to page 131.*
To go THROUGH THE DESERT, *turn to page 137*

THROUGH THE SWAMP—THE ART OF WAR

"The swamp is the fastest option, though I'm not sure it's the safest." Darzon pointed to the map splayed on the table. "It should only take you half a day to make it to the next camp."

"We should make the most of our time. I say we risk the swamp." Axen grabbed the map off the table before heading to pack the rest of his things.

Soon, we were headed out of the city, and I wondered how long it would be before I saw anything that looked like home again. Reaching the gate, I waved goodbye to the guard and followed Axen toward the edge of the valley. His feet stomped the ground as he walked.

"Something on your mind?" I asked.

"No."

"Are you sure? Because it looks like—"

Axen turned and his icy eyes blazed an electric current. "I'm fine," he spoke through his teeth.

"Okay," I mumbled. Keeping my mouth shut, I continued toward the swamp. *I wonder what has him so angry. And why do his eyes do that? What did the Answers do to him?* Quieting the voices, I focused on the journey ahead.

The stench of the swamp accosted my nose before the scraggly trees and moldy boulders came into view. My stomach churned as we approached the sea of mud.

Two spindly trees bent together, forming an entrance to what looked like a path. A post stuck in the mud to the right appeared to have writing on it. Getting closer, I read aloud.

"'What one sees as a strength can be his weakness.'" I looked to Axen. "What do you think that means?"

"I don't know. Just some silly proverb, I guess. But look, Darzon was right, you can see the camp from here. It's a straight shot through the swamp. This will save us some time."

Heading into the pathway, I pulled my jacket around my nose to try to filter the smell. The path split in two directions— one led straight, and the other, marked by a sign with an arrow, led off to the left.

"I think we should follow the sign." My voice sounded muffled in my coat.

"No way. This way is straight. Why would we go out of our way?"

I didn't argue, and we continued. Soon, another pathway veered off to the right, again with an arrow.

"Axen, I think we should go that way. It doesn't look like we're getting anywhere just going straight."

"That's crazy, Calessa. We aren't going to waste our time going the scenic route. Keep moving."

Hours passed and countless arrowed trails were left unexplored. Keeping my eye on the end of the swamp, I could tell we weren't making much progress.

"Axen, at this rate, we won't make it to the camp until sundown. Can we please just trust the signs?" My jaw started to set as I spoke. *He can be so stubborn.*

Axen turned with lightning in his eyes. "You learned you can read like a week ago, and now you think you know everything? Well, you don't. I have been through more than you could ever dream. You didn't even know there was an outside world until I showed it to you."

Lightning flickered through Axen's eyes, and I felt as if I was watching a miniature storm. The electric blue blocked out his pupils. What had the Answers done to him? Whatever it was looked painful.

"Axen, you need to calm down." I took a step toward him, but his rampage continued.

"You have no idea what I've been through, and yet you dare to question me on the simplest things!"

I barely heard his words as I watched his body begin to quiver as if an electrical current was running rampant in his veins.

"Axen, please. You need to cool off. Please, listen to me." I reached out to touch his arm, and a sharp jolt of electricity shocked me numb. I dropped to the muddy ground and cried out.

"Calessa!" The shock must have pulled Axen from his enraged state, and he knelt beside me. "I'm so sorry. I told you I was still infected. Are you okay?"

His eyes had softened once more.

"Yes, I'm okay. But do you mind telling me what just happened?" I stood on shaky legs and attempted to brush the muck from my pants.

"The Answers sent us through electromagnetic brain therapy. It's how they controlled us. They instilled thoughts into our mind and destroyed memories to create us into mindless drones. I managed to keep most of my wits, but I haven't quite detoxed from their ways of thinking. To them, anyone questioning them is an enemy." His voice dropped lower than his head as he looked down at his hands. "I'm sorry, Calessa. I should have told you all this sooner."

I placed my hand on his shoulder. "It's okay. I'm sure you've been through a lot." I pulled Axen to his feet and focused back on the path ahead. "I still think we need to try another path."

Axen sighed. "Okay, let's try that next one up there." We followed the next trail and soon lost sight of the camp.

However, after a few twists and turns, I saw another arrow turning us back toward the end. After only an hour, we had reached the end of the swamp. Looking like monsters covered in mud, we made our way to the camp where I could see a crowd gathered around a fire. It didn't take long for the group to notice us, their shoulders tensing at our approach.

Axen must have noticed, too, and raised his hands in a sign of surrender. "Hello!" he called. "We're not your enemies. Please don't be afraid."

The campers settled a bit, but the men kept their hands near their weapons.

"Who are you then?" a man yelled.

"We're friends of Aldred," I said.

They took their hands from their weapons and one man stepped forward.

"What brings you all the way out here?" he asked.

"Aldred sent us to find the Final Answer. I know we're close, but we're still searching. My name is Axen and this is Calessa."

The man shook Axen's hand, and an older woman stood to greet us.

"I knew Aldred years ago. How is that old man?" She smiled sweetly.

"We didn't get to spend much time with him, but he seemed good," I said.

"Well, that's nice." The woman's squinting eyes looked us over. "Now, before you two get to talking business, I believe we should get you out of those muddy clothes. Come along." She led us away and gave us fresh clothes to change into. The soft cotton felt like heaven after the sweat and grime I had been living in. Axen headed back to talk to the men, and I followed the woman.

"You said you knew Aldred. Do you know anything about the Final Answer?" I asked.

"Well, I can't say yes, and I can't say no. I have my own conspiracy theories but no way to prove them."

"The leader of the last camp said he believed the answer lies within the first letters of quotes left behind in classic novels. Each camp seems to have a different one. So far, the quotes have started with a T, a W, and an I. I'm not sure what to make of it though."

The old woman's eye lit up. "You, my dear, may have just proven my madness." She scurried over to a small bookshelf and pulled a book from its place. Bringing it over, she placed the book on her lap. "This is my ancestor's copy of *The Art of War* by Sun Tzu. There is a particular quote that had the first letter underlined." She leafed through the pages. "Ah! Here it is. It says, 'Appear weak when you are strong, and strong when you are weak.' I always thought the first letters may spell an author's name. The one author who has the Final Answer. So now, you can add an A to your list." She shut the book and returned it to its place.

"I hope Aldred will be able to help us decipher it all when we return. I don't know any authors."

The woman chuckled and went about washing our clothes. I wandered back outside to where Axen sat with the men, studying a map.

"Calessa, there you are. We have a map to the next camp."

"And I have our next quote." I sat next to him at a large wooden table and looked to see two paths leading to the next camp. One led through an underground mine and another showed an area marked as ruins. "Which way do you think we should go?"

"I'm not sure. But I think we should eat something before we decide."

***

To go THROUGH THE MINE, *turn to page 143*
To go THROUGH THE RUINS, *turn to page 149*

THROUGH THE FOREST—WAR AND PEACE

"I think we should stick to the forest. At least the terrain is something we're familiar with." Axen spoke as he gathered our things. His mood seemed to have to have brightened since being here.

"I agree," Darzon said. "You'll have the best luck going through the woods. I've heard it's beautiful there. Last scout we sent out said the trees were taller than our buildings, and the air was so fresh you couldn't drink enough in."

"That would be a nice change of pace."

I listened to the exchange between the men as I sipped on some tea Darzon had given me. As soon as I finished, we thanked our host and left. The sun was shining in the city, and I could feel the uplifted spirits around me in my heart. While this place may have looked like Ashkelan, there seemed to be a significant difference between the two. Laughter wafted from the street vendors and everyone seemed to have a smile on their lips rather than the dirty secrets Ashkelan held. You could almost feel the lightheartedness here rather than the oppression and control that Ashkelan brought.

Exiting the gate, I turned for one last look. *I think I would like living in a town like that. Though I could live anywhere that wasn't a prison.*

"Calessa, I think I owe you an explanation," Axen said as we made our way out of the valley.

I raised my eyebrows. "Explanation of what?"

"Of what happened to me. I think you should know about my time with the Answers."

"Okay, well, I know you were taken when you were twelve and whatever they did to you messed up your memories. What else should I know?"

"Well, you know how I told you I'm still infected?"

"Yes, I assume that's what causes the shockwave to go through your eyes? That looked painful."

"It is, but I've gotten used to it. It's because of the electromagnetic brain therapy they had us go through. Every day, I would be hooked up to machines. They sent shockwaves through my brain telling me how I should think and act, while stealing my memories in the process." Axen stopped for a moment and turned to me. "My mind was reprogramed. If I feel any emotion too strongly, the aftershocks of the therapy run wild in my body. It was the Answers' way of controlling us into submission. That's why I try to stay as level as possible. To avoid an episode." He turned and continued walking.

The voices talked through the information as I tried to think what to say. *That's terrible, but it explains a lot. No wonder he stays so emotionless. I'd hate to see what the aftershocks are like. And to think, that almost happened to me.*

"I'm sorry. No one should have to go through that." I tried to think of something more to say when I felt a shift in the air. "Axen, are we going the right way?"

"Uh, according to the map, yes. Why?"

"Something seems off." I noticed flakes falling from the sky, and I caught one in my hand. *It's not cold, so it's not snow.* I took a deep breath. Rather than the fresh air I was told came with the forest, my lungs were met with the burning of a breath of smoke. Something was on fire or had been. I looked at the fleck of ash in my hand. "I'm not so sure we're going to find the forest as refreshing as we thought."

As I spoke, we arrived at the top of the valley and I saw a horrible sight below. What had once been a forest, was now a wasteland. Charred remains took the place of trees, and the blue sky had been turned gray with soot and smoke.

"I guess we can forget about catching a break," Axen grumbled.

"Maybe so, but the fire is out. At least we can still go through the forest."

Walking toward the edge of the woods, my heart saddened at the sight. Black ash stuck to my fingers as I brushed my hand against the trunk of what was once a young tree. Wind whistled through the ghost of what used to be, and I could feel the smoky flurries catch in my hair.

"I wonder what happened," I said.

"I'm not sure. Probably a freak wildfire. We should be thankful it didn't reach the city," Axen responded.

"That's true. But this is awful. Everything's gone. There's no life left."

"It's sad, but there's nothing we can do about it. I say we keep moving."

I stepped into the forest, and my boots crunched through the debris. It was as if someone had drained all the color. Shades of gray left a solemn mood over the woods.

"It's sad that something so young and beautiful had to be destroyed." My voice echoed in the bare air.

"Well, that's kind of what it's like to be an Answer." Axen looked at me. "They took my mind away and tried to drain the life from me. I had to fight with everything I could. Kind of like this forest must have fought against the fire."

"But you at least still have hope, don't you? You managed to keep some of yourself."

"Yes, but something tells me this place has hope too." Axen walked deeper into the woods and knelt by a scraggly stump. "Look, here."

I walked over to see a small bud of green swirled from the base of the stump. A new life beginning.

"How is it growing in this condition?" I asked.

"It knows that if it tries hard enough, it can beat all the odds. Just like I am." Axen stood and continued forward. "I'll bet we see more of that before we make it out. Nature is resilient. It has many lessons to share."

My spirits lifted as we traveled along. The farther we walked the more green I saw. As if the universe was coloring itself in, the woods began to grow to more life. I could taste the fresher air as we went, the smoke dissipating.

Leaving the dreary sight behind us, Axen and I found our way to the edge of the wood and could see the camp not too far off. As we neared, a group of men and women surrounding a fire stood to meet us. Their hands on their weapons, the men created a shield in front of the women.

"Who are you?" a man called.

"We're friends. We've come from the base camp. We are searching for the Final Answer," I responded.

The men relaxed their stances and invited us over to the fire. An older woman gave us something to eat, and we filled the campers in on our travels so far.

"We do have a quote for you," the man said. "And I believe we have a map to the next nearest camp. Give me a minute." The man left and returned a moment later with a book in one hand and a piece of a map in the other.

"*War and Peace* by Leo Tolstoy," I read aloud as the man handed me the book.

"Yes, the quote inside says, 'As long as there is life, there is still happiness,'" the man said.

"So, now we can add an A to our list of letters," Axen said.

"What do you think it all means?" I asked.

The old woman spoke up. "I believe the first letters may spell out the name of the author who had access to the Final Answer. But I wouldn't be able to tell you which author that might be."

"Something tells me we don't have all the letters yet." Axen reached for the map the man brought and opened it up. "I think our best bet is to get to the next camp before nightfall."

"You should be able to." The man pointed to two trails. "You can go through these ruins here, though I can't tell you what kind of state they're in. It could be dangerous to go that way if you aren't careful. Your other option is to head over to a labyrinth that was built by our ancestors. Only readers can make it through, so it shouldn't be a problem for you two, though that way is a little longer of a trek."

"Which way do you think we should go?" I asked.

***

To go THROUGH THE RUINS, *turn to page 149*
To go THROUGH THE LABYRINTH, *turn to page 153*

OVER THE RIVER—GREAT EXPECTATIONS

"I think going across the river will cut back on time, and I'd like to make it to the next camp by midday." Axen finished his breakfast and stood. "I have a feeling we aren't too far from the Final Answer."

"I'll warn you the bridge that crosses the river is inhabited by a family of creatures. They look like what some may call goblins or trolls, but they don't take kindly to being called either," Darzon spoke as he cleared our plates.

"Then what are they?" I asked.

"No one knows for sure. But as long as you're respectful, they shouldn't give you any trouble."

"Well, let's hope they're in pleasant moods today."

I gathered my things, and Axen and I thanked Darzon for his hospitality. Walking back through the city in the morning light brought back memories of Ashkelan. The high walls cast dark shadows and the bustle of people milling around brought both the calm sense of familiar with a cringe of feeling trapped. Reaching the gate, I felt happy to leave the city. The wide-open world was much more appealing. It didn't take long to find the river, however, there was no bridge in sight.

"How far down is the bridge?" I asked, peeking over Axen's shoulder at the map.

"I'm not sure. The map isn't too clear on distance. I hope it won't be too far."

The warm sun melted my tense muscles of the days before, and I relaxed into our journey. "What was it like back at Answers Headquarters?" I asked.

"You don't want to know," Axen said with a scoff.

"I do, though. I would have been inducted too if you hadn't found me. I want to know what it was like. Please?"

"Okay, fine. The Answers only wanted minions. Anyone who could go against them was automatically an enemy. That's why they took us as soon as we knew we could read. Personally, I think they set up the secret library as a trap. They knew we kids played inside the tower. Trust me, if they had wanted to catch us, they could have."

"So, they were watching us the whole time?"

"Yes, they have cameras hidden to watch what was going on in the tower. They watch to see how someone reacts when they find the library. If they suspect that person can read, they capture them. That's why the guards were hot on your trail as soon as you figured it out."

"Wait, how did you know they were close?" I stopped Axen and turned him around. "Were you watching me?"

Axen blushed. "Yes, I was. I could see the library through a vent in the hidden tunnel. I heard someone in there and stopped to watch. You got a look in your eyes, and I knew you'd heard the voices for the first time. That's why I ran to the panel to rescue you. I figured you'd have nowhere to go, and I didn't want the Answers to get another member." He turned away and continued walking.

I stood for a moment, taking it all in, and then rushed to catch up.

"Well, thank you," I said. "I don't know what would have happened to me if you hadn't been there."

"I do. The guards would have taken you. You would have been put into electromagnetic therapy, and you would have forgotten you could read by the end of the day."

"Wow. That's intense. Wait. Then how did you get through and still be able to read?"

"I didn't. I forgot my first day too. But I was a little more adventurous than the other minions and would go exploring. I found the library and remembered all over again—this time avoiding the cameras. After that, I would keep a note in my pocket to remind myself every time I got out of the therapy."

"How did you get the note? Wait! You can write?" My mind spun with all the information.

"Yes. I trained myself to copy the words I saw in books. It's not so hard once you know what they say."

"I can't believe it. What do the Answers even want with us anyway? Why do they care?"

"Well, readers have been said to have power beyond human control. The Answers don't like not being in control, so they decided to put an end to us. What they don't understand is they will never destroy readers. Words have more power than they could ever know." Axen pointed ahead. "Look, there's the bridge."

I let the voices try to sort through all the new information and looked where Axen pointed. Not too far down the river, a huge wooden bridge crossed to the other side. The sides looked peculiar and, as we approached, I saw they were etched with various pictures of creatures but saw no sign of the inhabitants Darzon had warned us about.

"Maybe the creatures aren't home?"

Before he could respond, I noticed some of the moss moving around the bank of the river. Shivering like the fur of a beast, the moss began to rise. The rocks and mud underneath formed a lumpy body, and a grumpy face appeared.

"Who you calling creatures?" the beast grumbled.

I stammered as I took in the sight. "I-I'm sorry. I didn't mean any disrespect."

The beast smiled a mouthful of pebbles and wobbled over to us. "Well, in that case, welcome! My name's Jaki.

And this is my wife, Looka. The kids are playing down the way." As he talked, another creature formed from the mud, this one with a what I could only call "moss-hair."

"Hello. I'm Calessa, and this is Axen. We were hoping to cross the bridge. Would that be all right?"

"Yes, of course." Jaki moved in front of the entrance, blocking our way.

I looked to Axen, who seemed just as confused. "Well, then," Axen said, "I guess we'll be on our way. Will you let us pass?"

"Why, certainly," Looka said. Hobbling next to her husband, they created a blockade.

"I thought you said we were allowed to pass?" I asked.

"Oh, you are, dear," Looka said.

I tried to slip past them, but Jaki stuck out his root-like leg, tripping me.

"Hey! Let us through!" My ears turned hot.

Looka and Jaki split and made a path between them. Cautious, I inched toward them. They stood as still as the stones they were, and I passed them without an issue. Axen followed and we breathed a sigh of relief. We started to cross and soon noticed the two creatures had begun to follow us.

"Why are you following us?" I asked, turning around.

"We thought we'd walk with you." Looka grabbed my hand, forcing me to slow my pace.

"I appreciate the offer, but we really need to hurry."

"Oh, well, all right." Looka changed the pace and soon we were all but running down the bridge.

I looked at Axen for help, but he was being dragged by Jaki down the bridge in the opposite direction.

"Where are you going?" I yelled.

"Nowhere, dear," Looka said.

"I wasn't talking to you! Axen! What's going on?"

"I asked him about what we should call them, and he started dragging me. I don't know how to stop a solid rock!" Axen tried to pull away from Jaki, but the roots had tangled around his ankles.

My face flushed. I turned to Looka who was still trying to race to the end of the bridge. "Looka, stop!" I yelled. Almost face planting, Looka stopped mid-step. The voices began chattering in my head. *They don't like questions. Tell them what to do and they listen.*

"Axen, tell Jaki to bring you this way!" I listened as Axen did what I said. Jaki turned and practically carried Axen to where I stood. I looked at our two new acquaintances and spoke as clearly as I could. "Jaki, Looka, thank you for letting us pass. Now go home and leave us be." The two beasts chittered for a moment and then waved goodbye, wobbling their way back to the bank of the river.

"How did—"

I clamped a hand over Axen's mouth. "Don't ask any questions."

His eyebrows raised, but he remained quiet as we made our way across the bridge. Reaching the end, I could see the camp. We wandered toward it and soon saw that it was almost as busy as the city. A man came to greet us as we neared. After telling them our story, the campers welcomed us in.

As we sat down for some lunch, an older woman came to our side. "I hear you want the Final Answer," she said as she lay a book in front of us. "Well, I happen to know part of the answer lies within these pages. The quotes you seek spell the name of the author by which the Final Answer is kept. Here is your next clue."

I pulled the book over. *Great Expectations* by Charles Dickens. I opened it to where a piece of a map had been stuck between the pages and read the quote aloud as Axen snatched the parchment. "'Ask no questions and you'll be told no lies.'"

Axen snorted as he looked at the map. "I wish someone had told us that a few hours ago." The campers looked at us in confusion. "Never mind. Looks like the next camp isn't too far off. We can go through this labyrinth here or head down to that bog there. Calessa?" He looked at me.

***

To go THROUGH THE LABYRINTH, *turn to page 153*
To go THROUGH THE BOG, *turn to page 159*

THROUGH THE SPARSE WOODS—
THE CALL OF THE WILD

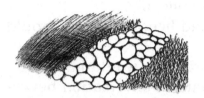

"I think we should go through the woods." Axen pushed his breakfast plate aside and stood.

"That's a good idea. The jungle might be a tricky journey." Darzon helped me pack our things as he spoke. "I would still be cautious going through the woods, though. You never know what can lurk in shadows."

"I think we'll survive." Axen placed a hand on my shoulder but then pulled back.

His warm touch made my cheeks warm. "Uh, yeah," I stammered. "We'll be fine. Though I guess we should be on our way."

As we ventured back toward the main gate, my inner voice chattered. *I wonder what would have happened if I had been captured by the Answers. Would I have met Axen? What if Axen had never been caught? Would I have known him then? I wonder if the Answer's minions can even get to know each other. Would he have been the same?*

My thoughts continued to whirl as we exited the gate and headed out of the valley. I watched the way Axen moved and how he mumbled to himself as he followed the map. He had a way of being intimidating and endearing all at once.

"Axen, do you remember your family at all?" I asked.

"No, not really. I vaguely remember having one, but that's about it."

"So, you don't remember anything from your life before the Answers?"

"Nope."

"Wow. That must be hard." I thought for a moment before phrasing my next question. "Do the Answers have relationships?"

"What do you mean?"

"Like, if I had been inducted, would I have gotten to know you?"

"Well, we probably would have met, but the Answers don't support much conversation between minions. They know that conversations lead to relationships, and they think the feelings that come with that could produce an uprising."

"So, no one talks to each other?"

"Not really. And honestly, I don't blame them. Relationships are messy and cause more trouble than they're worth."

I stopped for a moment, and something within me sank a little. "Oh ... I see."

Axen turned back to look at me, and his face fell. "But maybe I'm being a hard shell." He searched my face for another moment and then turned back to the path.

I walked alongside his tall frame and considered his words. "How did they steal your memories anyway? That sounds impossible."

"Electromagnetic therapy."

"Sounds painful," I said, catching a glimpse of electricity flash through his ice-stormed eyes.

"It was. But they couldn't keep me from the library. I would hide notes for myself. Every time I had to go into a session, I would find a reminder about how I could read. I'd go and read as many books as I could from the library, making notes of what I read before I would be caught. Somehow, I started to train my mind to not let the therapy reach me, as well. Soon, I didn't need the notes, and I was able to retain information between sessions."

"That seems awful." I looked ahead and noticed the woods looming nearby.

The forest was indeed sparse, but the spindly trees reached taller than Axen. Walking closer, I noticed that most of the plants were young and barely able to hold themselves up.

"It looks like someone planted this forest on purpose." I looked at the rows of poplars and oaks.

"You're right, it does." Axen stepped onto a path.

"Who do you think did this?" I asked. "And why?"

"I don't know, but something seems off." Axen grabbed my hand. The rough callouses of his fingers brushed my skin, and I held tight. "Follow me and try to stay quiet. I don't trust these woods."

Walking along the trail, I tried to adjust my mind to the environment around me. The rustling leaves and the sound of the thin branches willowing in the breeze sounded almost like music. Even the chirps of some nearby birds seemed to stay in tune with the rhythm.

Dazed by nature's lullaby and Axen's hand in mine, I didn't notice the terrain changing beneath my feet until a sharp pain shot through my shoe. The soft moss had been replaced by pebbles and stone.

"Axen, look!"

Letting go of my hand, Axen looked down and frowned. Clearly, he had been as entranced as I had been.

"That's odd. But what about it? The road is just different here."

"Something doesn't seem right about it, though. I think we should stay off the path." I stepped off and regretted my decision.

The ground sank beneath my feet causing a sink hole to form. I lost my footing and could feel myself falling.

"Axen!"

Axen fell to his stomach on the still formed path and his strong arm grasped mine as I dangled in thin air.

"I've got you." Axen grunted as he tried to lift me back to safety. He pulled but could not lift my dead weight.

Some stones fell from the trail and sailed past my head into the abyss. The path was going to collapse.

"Axen, you have to let go. The road is about to fall. Get out of here before we both die! Someone has to find the Final Answer."

A sweat broke out on Axen's brow as his eyes bore into mine. "I'm not going anywhere without you."

Before my mind could analyze what he'd said, the trail crumbled beneath him, and we both plummeted into the darkness. Screaming, I gripped onto Axen's arm as he pulled me close. Much sooner than I expected, we hit the ground, hard. I landed on top of Axen but couldn't see in the pitch black. His hand snaked into my hair, and I felt my face flush.

"I thought you didn't believe in relationships?" I whispered, still trying to catch my breath.

"Like I said, maybe I was being a hard shell."

Axen pressed his lips on mine. The blood rushed through me, and a small zap of electricity shocked my body as we kissed. As we parted, I realized the electricity had done much more than just make our moment special, it had somehow powered this underground tunnel in which we had landed.

Small lanterns now lit a path that ended in a small amount of sunlight. Scrambling off Axen, I tried to regain my composure. He stood and, without another word, grabbed my hand as we walked toward the exit. Staying close to him, we reached the daylight and saw the camp not too far ahead.

"I guess you're glad you found me before escaping, huh?" I teased.

"Nah, you're just lucky I thought you were pretty." A smirk lit up his eyes.

An old woman met us outside the camp and, after a quick

round of introductions, led us into her home for some dinner. Her eyes grew wide as we spoke of our trip.

"I know the Final Answer you seek belongs to an author of old," she said as she hobbled to a bookshelf. "These clues will not tell you the answer itself, but rather the name of the one who holds it. Here is your next clue." She handed a book to me and I read the title.

"*The Call of the Wild* by Jack London." As I flipped to the marked page, a piece of parchment fell to the floor. Axen picked it up as I read the underlined quote. "'For the last time in his life, he allowed passion to usurp cunning and reason.'" I blushed, remembering the earlier events, and tried to distract myself by looking at what Axen had retrieved.

A new piece of a map stretched out on the table in front of us. A triangle marked the spot of a camp not too far off from our present location. A large building stood between the two camps.

"You can go straight through that old mansion if you'd like." The old woman pointed to the penciled drawing. "Or if you think you'd rather stay outside, you could go through the garden on the grounds instead. Either way should allow you to make it to your next clue by sundown."

I looked to Axen as he studied the map. "Which way do you think we should go?"

***

To go THROUGH THE MANSION, *turn to page 165*
To go THROUGH THE GARDEN, *turn to page 171*

THROUGH THE JUNGLE—THE JUNGLE BOOK

"Let's go through the jungle. I'd rather stay as hidden as possible." Axen scarfed down his breakfast between words.

"Those jungles can be dangerous," Darzon said. "But I don't see you having any trouble making it through by lunch."

I gathered my things and walked over to the table where the boys sat. "Maybe we'll find the answer today." I tried to sound optimistic.

"It's possible," Darzon replied. "I have a feeling you two are right on the tip of the truth. I can't thank you enough for all the work you're putting into this."

"Well, trust me, as someone who has seen what the Answers can do, I promise you this answer is our only hope." Axen grabbed his bag, threw his jacket over his shoulder, and looked at me. "Ready?"

"Ready."

I thanked Darzon and we headed out. I couldn't be happier to be leaving the walled city. The high walls brought back some unwelcome memories and I didn't like the feeling of being caged.

"Do you remember anything about growing up in Ashkelan?" I asked Axen.

"Not really. All I remember is what I learned from the books in the library."

"How did you manage not to get caught? Wait ... I thought they erased your memories. How did you know to go back to the library?"

"Well, the electromagnetic therapy they put me through did take my memories, but it didn't affect my wits. I would leave myself notes as to where to find the library, as well as how to avoid being caught. Each session was a little easier as I gained more knowledge, and my powers as a reader grew."

"That sounds exhausting."

"It was, but I knew one day I would escape, and it would all be worth it."

"So, I guess I got lucky that you happened to see me before you left." I playfully hit Axen in the arm as we passed through the front gates of the city.

"Actually, if I'm being honest, I saw you in the library. I was passing through the part of the tunnel that ran behind it when I heard you. I knew if I didn't help you, you'd be caught. Plus, I thought you were pretty cute." Axen's face turned red.

"You think I'm cute?" I felt my face flush as well and I stopped Axen with a hand on his arm.

"Uh ... yeah, I do." He turned away and started to walk at a brisk pace. I chose not to press the issue and lagged behind as we traveled through the valley.

I guess I was right about him maybe having feelings too. I smiled to myself as we went. *I guess almost getting caught by the Answers was a blessing in disguise.* I caught up to Axen's long strides.

"For what it's worth, I think you're pretty cute too," I mumbled.

Axen stopped and his bright eyes flashed. I guess I had stumped him on what to say. Rather than speak, he reached out for my hand, and we continued to the top of the valley.

As we looked out over the nearby land, I contemplated his hand in mine—rough and yet soft. I could see the jungle up ahead. The turquoise leaves of the tall trees seemed a vibrant contrast to the greenery of the valley behind.

Axen and I trod carefully as we walked into the midst of tangled vines and marshy floor. The dense nature of the jungle made it difficult to see where we were headed. Birds of all kinds floated above, their bright, colored wings catching in the sparse streams of sunlight. I could hear rustling in the bushes around us and the scurrying of small animals near our feet. Soon, the playful energy of the air changed, and I heard a noise I knew signaled trouble.

"Did you hear that growl?" I whispered.

"Yes. Stay low and quiet."

Axen pulled me down, and we began to creep along the path, our backs hunched as we slinked along.

Another growl followed, and I could hear a loud rustling to our right. A dark movement cut through the brush. I gasped, and Axen pulled me a little closer. A noise to the left grabbed my attention as the growling grew louder. Something stalked us, but the question was from which side. Axen turned and pressed his back to mine and we began to circle slowly, searching for the source of the danger. Soon, a large, striped cat erupted from within the trees and lunged toward us, its sharp teeth almost as large as its knife-like claws.

I screamed and closed my eyes, preparing for the attack. When I heard the beast yelp, I opened my eyes and saw another form hovering over the tiger. The creature pinned the cat to the ground, snarling in its face before releasing it and letting the tiger escape. The form turned to us, and Axen and I gasped.

A man covered from head to toe in mud and dirt stared back at us with wild eyes.

"Who are you?" I asked.

"I'm an Answer." The man took a step toward us, and both Axen and I backed away. "No, please." The man tried to catch his breath. "I'm a fugitive. I escaped from the Answers over a year ago." He put his hand out in surrender, and I took a step closer.

"What are you doing out here in the jungle?" I asked.

"I didn't know where to go once I escaped. All I know is I can read, and I don't know how, and I have these voices in my head. The Answers tried to take my memories and my mind, but I fought back and managed to get out. But I had no one to go to, and so I started to wander. Eventually, I ended up here and was able to build myself a home. I haven't spoken to another human being since I left."

"You mean you don't know about the other readers?" I glanced at Axen.

"There are more like me?" the man asked.

"We have a lot to tell you. Why don't you come with us?"

We started back through the jungle and soon reached the edge. After we filled the man in on everything, he agreed to come to the camp with us. Only an hour or so passed before we reached it, and an old woman came to greet us.

"Look what the jungle drug in." Her voice sounded sweet as she invited us in. After introductions and a quick overview of our journey, however, the old woman frowned. "You three look like you could use a hot meal before you go on your way." Fixing some lunch, the woman told us everything she knew of the Final Answer. "And finally," she said, "I know the clues you have been receiving will spell the name of the author that holds the Final Answer. And something tells me you two are close to the truth."

"Do you have a quote for us?" Axen asked.

The woman pointed to a book on a shelf and I picked it up. *The Jungle Book* by Rudyard Kipling. I flipped to a marked page and handed a piece of a map that fell out to Axen as I read the quote. "'For the strength of the pack is in the wolf, and the strength of the wolf is in the pack.'"

"Well, that adds an F to our list." Axen studied the map. "It looks like the next camp isn't too far off. We can either go through what looks to be a ghost town left from the old world or back through some of the forest."

"If it's all right with you," the young fugitive spoke up, "I think I'll stay here."

***

To go THROUGH THE GHOST TOWN, *turn to page 177*
To go THROUGH THE WOODS, *turn to page 183*

***

THROUGH THE MOUNTAIN PASS— JANE EYRE

"Let's take the mountain pass. I don't have the energy to be climbing all day," I said, rubbing the sleep from my eyes.

"That is the safest route," Darzon said.

Axen nodded as he packed our things.

"Darzon, do you know anything else about the Final Answer?" I asked.

"Only that the Final Answer isn't something the author has written, but rather something they've said."

"So, only a descendant of the author will even be able to know the answer," Axen stated, joining us at the table.

"Yes, precisely. And you two are very close to finding the descendant. The author only left five clues behind. You're more than halfway there." Darzon cleared our breakfast dishes. "But you two better be on your way. You should be able to reach the next camp by noon."

Axen and I thanked Darzon and headed out. Leaving his large house, I felt a sense of familiar as I stepped onto the cobblestone streets. *I wonder if I'll ever get home. I wonder if I even want to get home.*

We walked toward the gate and waved to the guard as we passed through. Stepping beyond the walls, I felt a wave of relief ride in on the fresh morning air. I breathed deep and faced the edge of the valley.

"Do you think you'll ever go back to Ashkelan?" Axen asked.

"I'm not sure. I don't think so."

"Well, don't you have family there?"

"I have my sister. I suppose I would have to go back for her. But I'd bring her back out here with me. I can't live within those walls forever. Not when I know what the world is like."

"What happened to your parents?"

"Mom's dead, and Dad's dead to me." I glared at the grass below, unwilling to look at Axen.

"I'm sorry about your mom. Do you want to talk about it?"

"No." For the first time on this trip, I wanted silence as we trekked up the valley.

"Well, I'm still sorry." Axen sidled up next to me. "Do you remember anything about my family?"

My heart softened. *How can I be so selfish? At least I remember my family. Even if one of them is a scumbag.*

"I'm sorry, Axen. I wasn't even thinking about the fact that you don't know your family." I sighed. "All I can tell you is you had a sister. She used to play with my sister when we were kids. But after you disappeared, your parents wouldn't let her come out anymore. They were afraid to lose her too."

Axen furrowed his brow for a moment before his eyes lit up. "I remember her. She always looked up to me when we were kids. And now she must think I'm dead." His eyes went dark again.

"Well, hopefully soon, you'll be able to go find her. And your parents. I'm sure they'll be thrilled to see you." I placed a hand on Axen's arm.

"I guess I should be focusing on what's ahead rather than behind." Axen pointed as we hit the top of the valley. "Speaking of which, I think I've found our passageway."

Huge boulders marked the entrance to the pass, and we headed in that direction. I tilted my head, trying to see the top of the mountain. Pebbles and stones trickle down the sides as we reached the base.

"I'm glad we didn't decide to climb," I said, shielding my eyes from the morning sun.

"Well, let's get moving. It'll take longer to navigate the pass, and I still hope to make it to the camp by lunch."

Axen stepped onto the path, and I followed. It seemed peaceful within the rock tunnel until we heard a loud boom from around a bend.

"What was that?" Another thunderous noise covered my words. Axen stepped around the corner and then backed slowly to me.

"Stay quiet. We've got visitors." He motioned to follow him.

As we peeked around the corner, I saw two beings almost as large as the mountain itself.

"They're giants," Axen whispered.

The loud booms were clearer here, and it didn't take long for me to realize the noise was the monstrous voices of the giants yelling at one another. I tried to listen to what they were saying, but the sonic booms almost didn't register in my ears.

I was about to ask Axen how to get around them when I saw something that caused me to pause. Looking up, I could see chunks of the mountain face shaking loose from the earth-shattering noise. The giants were going to cause an avalanche. I pointed to the rocks, and Axen followed my gaze.

"We have to get them to stop yelling," I said.

"And how do you expect to get their attention?"

"Like this." I ran out into the opening, waving my arms and yelling at the top of my lungs. "Hey! Over here!"

The giants kept arguing. I realized this wasn't going to be as simple as I thought. I walked right in between the two towering beings and kicked the one's big toe.

"Hey!" I shouted. "Down here!" The giants stopped their roaring and looked down.

"Who are you?" one giant said. Its voice sounded calmer but was still obnoxiously loud.

"I'm Calessa, and you two almost killed us all. Look!" I pointed to the loosening rocks.

The giants gasped, causing another cavalcade of debris. They clapped their hands over their mouths to keep from talking and knelt.

"Thank you." The giant's whisper still sounded like a shout.

"You're welcome," I said. "Next time you two get into an argument, maybe take it somewhere that wouldn't cause mortal danger."

"Yes, ma'am." The giants looked as sheepish as giants could and stomped off, passing Axen as they went.

"How did you do that?" Axen asked as he made his way over to me.

"I have no idea." I let out a breath I hadn't known I was holding. "I took a risk and it paid off."

"You could've been killed in multiple ways." Axen's eyes were big with what I could only assume was shock. Either that or he was impressed.

"Guess it's good I wasn't then, right?" I turned and started down the trail. Reaching the end of the pass, I could see the camp in the distance. "Ready to get our next clue?" I asked.

Axen nodded and we headed toward the camp. An old woman came to greet us.

"And who might you two be?" she asked with a sweet smile.

"I'm Axen, and this is Calessa." Axen filled the woman in on our journey.

"Well, I do believe I have a clue. Follow me." The woman led us to her tent and offered us something to eat as she retrieved a book from a shelf. She handed it to us, and I looked at the cover. *Jane Eyre* by Charlotte Brontë. Opening the book, I turned to a page marked with parchment and read the underlined quote.

"'Life appears to me too short to be spent in nursing animosity or registering wrongs.'" I looked at Axen, but he was already unfolding the parchment which happened to be a piece of a map.

"You should be able to reach the next camp yet today if you hurry," the old woman said. "You can either go through the winter forest or by the old training course where the Answers trained their first minions."

"Well," I looked at Axen. "Which way?"

***

To go THROUGH THE WINTER FOREST, *turn to page 189*
To go THROUGH THE TRAINING COURSE, *turn to page 195*

OVER THE MOUNTAIN—THE GREAT GATSBY

"Seeing how long the mountain path is, going over the mountain may actually cut back on time." Axen packed our things as I finished my breakfast.

I turned to Darzon. "Do you have anything else you could tell us about the Final Answer before we leave?"

"Well, only a descendant of the author will know the answer. It won't be written in a book but rather something passed down from generation to generation," Darzon said.

"But why wouldn't the author have broken the brainwashing while they were still alive?" I asked.

"They knew the world would resort back to its evil ways." Darzon sighed. "I can only assume that's why it has been kept a secret this long, waiting for the right people to find it."

"And how do we know we're the right people?" Axen scrutinized the map he held in his hands.

"You two prove there's hope for Ashkelan and the rest of us. As far as I know, you two are the only ones that have escaped and been able to navigate the realms to find these clues."

"I hope we can live up to that standard," I said.

"I'm sure you will." Darzon led us to the door. "Now, be careful and hopefully the next time I see you, the world will be free again. You two are very close to the end. Only five clues are needed to know the author's name." We thanked our host and then headed back through the town, waving to the guard as we passed the gate.

"I can easily say, after spending a night in that city, I never want to be trapped inside walls again," I said as I breathed in the fresh morning breeze.

"Why's that? Didn't you like growing up in Ashkelan?"

"No. My mother died when I was young, but I inherited her sense of adventure. Something my father never understood. I somehow always knew there had to be something more."

"I'm sorry about your mother." Axen sighed. "I'm hoping when we get back, I might be able to find my family. I remember having one, so I know they exist. Though they probably think I'm dead by now."

"A lot of the families that lost kids became more reclusive afterwards. I don't even remember your family, if I'm honest, though I think you had a sister."

Axen's eyes sparkled for a moment. "I did! She's younger than me. I remember that now."

"Well, do you think you'll move back once this is all over?"

"I doubt it. I'm like you. I don't think I could ever be happy trapped in a city again. I need the wide-open space."

"Who knows, maybe they'll knock down the walls once the Answers are eliminated. There won't be a reason to have them anymore anyway."

"That's true. I wouldn't be surprised if that's the first thing people do. I wouldn't wait to knock down some walls if I knew a whole world was on the other side."

Axen and I reached the top of the valley and looked ahead. My eyes focused in on the mountain range not too far off, and I headed in that direction.

"Any ideas on how we're going to get up that mountain?" I asked.

"I have a few," Axen replied.

Nearing the base, I shielded my eyes and looked up. The mountains reached high and looked as treacherous as I had feared. Shale made for a delicate siding to the mountain face, and the obvious footholds were few and far between.

"Okay, mastermind, how are we getting up this thing?" I turned and saw Axen pulling ropes and picks from his bag. He tossed me a rope and I tied it around my middle as he attached a pick to the other end and did the same to his.

"Toss the pick as high as you can and try to snag it in the rocks. We can climb part way up, and then find a foothold to stand on while we toss the pick up again."

It sounded simple in theory, but I had a bad feeling this was going to be much more difficult than planned. Tossing my rope high, I watched as it clanged back down next to me. *Well, this isn't going well. Maybe I'll go through the pass after all and leave him to this crazy adventure.* I tossed it a few more times and was about to give up when the pick finally caught. I tugged to make sure it was secure.

"Okay, now what?" I turned to see that Axen had been watching me the whole time and appeared to be holding back a chuckle. I glared at him and he cleared his throat.

"Okay." He looked up the mountainside. "Start climbing. If you fall, you're tied to the pick. There's a foothold not too far from where yours landed. Get to it and find your balance."

I did as he said, earning a few scrapes along the way. Reaching the foothold by my pick, I stopped and clung to the mountain wall. A few moments later, Axen stopped next to me and pulled my pick from the shale. Tossing it again, much higher than I could have, the pick dug into the mountain on his first try. He motioned for me to keep going. After several tosses of the pick, we soon reached the top of the cliff, exhausted but relieved.

A long path winded across the top of the mountain, and I sighed in relief when I saw that it continued in a nice grade down the other side. I was about to comment on the easy descent when I heard a voice cry out from the side of the mountain. Walking over to the outer edge, I looked down to see a man lying on a ledge below.

"Please, help!" he called.

"What happened?" I yelled back.

"I'm a scout from the nearby camp. I was sent out to find the next camp north when I fell off the cliff. Something within the mountain range caused an earthquake, and I lost my balance."

I could see he was badly bruised, and his leg bent away from his body in an unnatural way.

"You're hurt. Can you stand?" I asked.

"No, I think I broke my leg. I've been here three days and ran out of food and water long before the first day had passed. Please, you've got to help me."

Axen pulled me back from the edge and looked at me with cold eyes. "We can't help him."

"Why not?" I scowled. "We can't leave him there to die."

"We would be risking our lives trying to rescue him, and for all we know, it's a trap and he's an Answer in disguise."

I yanked my arm out of his grip. "That's enough. I'm helping him, whether you like it or not." I walked back to the edge and looked down at the injured man. Turning to Axen, I mumbled. "But I could use your help."

He sighed. "Fine. But if this turns out badly, I'm blaming you."

Axen stuck my pick into the ground and showed me how to rappel down the side of the mountain. After I reached the ledge, I wrapped my rope around the man and helped him sit in the makeshift sling. Axen started to pull us up, and I did my best to help. It didn't take long for us to reach the top, and I pulled us over the edge. As we caught our breath, Axen put our climbing supplies away.

"Thank you," the man said. "Though, I may need some assistance to get down the mountain."

Helping the man hop on one foot, we made our way down the winding path to the base of the mountain. I could see the camp ahead, and the man urged us to head straight for it.

"They know me, so there shouldn't be a problem," he said.

As we made our way into the camp, an old woman ran out to greet us.

"Oh my! What happened to you?" She looked at the young man.

"Sorry, Grandma." He winced as he tried to put weight on his broken leg.

"Well, sorry isn't going to fix that leg. Come on. And who might you two saviors be?" She glanced our way as she led us to her tent.

"I'm Calessa, and this is Axen." I explained our situation and how we came about her grandson while she went to work doctoring the man.

"Well, dears, as soon as I get my boy here to the doctor, I'll be back to chat. I believe I might have what you're looking for." The old woman helped the young man out the door, leaving Axen and me to sit and wait. Not too long passed before she returned and scurried over to a bookshelf.

"Here is my ancestor's copy of *The Great Gatsby* by F. Scott Fitzgerald. You'll find your clue, as well as a map to the next camp, tucked inside."

I opened the book and handed the map to Axen as I read. "'Let us learn to show our friendship for a man when he is alive and not after he is dead.'" I looked over Axen's shoulder at the map.

"You can get to the camp through an old Answers training course or by way of the enchanted village. The choice is yours. But first, let me get you two something to eat." The old woman hobbled over to her kitchen.

***

ONCE UPON A BOOK

To go THROUGH THE TRAINING COURSE, *turn to page 195*
To go THROUGH THE ENCHANTED VILLAGE, *turn to page* 201

THROUGH THE DESERT—LES MISÉRABLES

"I'd rather stay on a flat plain. I don't have the energy to climb a mountain today." I finished my breakfast and helped Darzon clear the dishes.

"But going over the mountain will cut a few hours off our journey," Axen piped up from the living area.

"Axen, please. I'm tired and sore."

"I think we should take the quickest route."

"Axen, no. We're taking the desert trail. I'm not dealing with a treacherous climb today."

"You should still be able to reach the next camp by noon," Darzon chimed in. "And I'll let you know, you two are close to the author's name. You only need five letters to complete it. Though I wouldn't waste too much time, I feel the world is losing hope."

"And how are we any symbol of hope?" I asked. The wear of the journey was starting to get to me. "I'm just a girl who can read, and Axen is a fugitive."

"You two have shown courage and love for our world by escaping the Answers and trying to find the Final Answer. I know it has brought hope to the readers of this city. I can only imagine it was the same for the camps before this."

"Well, I don't think any of it counts until we find the answer completely." Axen packed our things. "But I think it's time to head out. Darzon, thank you for your hospitality and advice."

"Yes, thank you. You've given us more than enough information," I said.

After saying goodbye, we headed out into the morning light. The city looked warm in the glow, giving it a hominess I'd never felt within Ashkelan's walls. *Maybe you could stay here. It looks like home but is much nicer. Maybe this whole trip has been too much. I can't be the world's only hope.*

My internal voice continued to rant as we passed through the city square and headed through the gate. Looking up the valley, I had a feeling today wasn't going to be as simple as we hoped. The mountain range stretched into the sky. Even at this distance, I had to crane my neck to see the top. I trudged in silence alongside an equally grumpy Axen.

"Fine. We'll take the desert," Axen spoke through his teeth.

"Good." I took a deep breath. "So, what do you think we'll need to do once we find the Final Answer?"

"I don't know. I would assume it'll involve getting back into the city, though."

"Any ideas on how we'll do that?"

"No. I only knew of the one tunnel, and the Answers are sure to have it guarded now that they know we escaped through there."

"Well, maybe Aldred will know a way in. And we still don't even know who the descendant is. For all we know, that could take years to figure out." My mind started to overload, and I felt the heat rising in my head.

"Well, we don't have much time, so let's hope we can figure it out quickly."

My brain stopped whirling at Axen's statement, and I stared at him. "What do you mean we don't have much time?"

"The Answers are building an army of drones. Any of the minions that rebel get put in the testing facility for new therapy techniques and usually end up coming out brainless. The Answers can tell them anything and they will oblige. They plan on attacking the city."

"When?"

"I don't know, but last I checked, they wanted an army of one thousand before they did."

"And how many did they have when you left?"

"988. And they have at least one rebel a week."

I mentally screamed but managed to keep my face solemn. "I guess we better have the hope that Darzon was talking about then."

We reached the top of the valley, and I could see the desert stretching out before us. The sand shimmered with heat as the sun beat down on it.

"You remembered to bring water, right?" I asked.

"Who would forget water when they know they're going to a desert?"

Axen's sarcastic tone did not strike well, and my mood worsened.

This is not going well, my inner voice complained as we walked closer to the desert edge. Stepping onto the sand, I waited for the heat to radiate into my boots, but it felt cool. Something in the air caught my eye and I looked up. Small flakes fell all around me. I reached out a hand and caught one. A tiny kiss of cold touched my skin before dissolving.

"Snow in a desert?" I wondered aloud. "Just our luck." As the flurries picked up, I noticed the temperature drop and realized maybe we wouldn't need the water after all.

"How is this even possible?" Axen griped. "The sun has been blaring all morning." His eyes turned into a storm as he looked at me.

"Well, don't look at me! It's not my fault it's snowing!" The flurries turned to a squall as large flakes started coming down in droves.

"Well, do you have any suggestions on how to get through a desert in a snowstorm?"

The squall turned into a blizzard, and I could barely see Axen standing three feet away. The snow grew heavier and the wind blew wildly. Wrapping my arms around my middle to try to retain heat, I made my way closer to Axen.

"We need to start moving," I yelled, hoping my voice would reach over the roar of the wind.

"We can't even see two feet ahead. How are we supposed to make it through?"

"If we stand still, we'll freeze to death." The snow began to lay on the ground, and after a few moments, had risen to our calves. I had never seen a blizzard this bad.

"This never would have happened if we had climbed the mountain like I'd wanted!" I could see the electricity blitz through Axen's eyes as he yelled.

"Well, I'm sorry for trying to make our trip a little easier!" My inner temperature rose.

"Well, this isn't easier!" Axen turned and started to trudge through the now knee-deep snow. It didn't take long for him to lose balance, and he faceplanted into the drift.

I gasped but then couldn't help but laugh. Snickering soon turned to a belly laugh as Axen stood and faced me. His body covered in white powder, he looked like a living snowman.

The snow abruptly stopped. Looking around, I saw that the snow coated the entire desert, including the tumbleweeds and most of the cacti around the area, but no new flakes fell.

"How did you make it stop?" Axen's face turned red as he brushed the snow from his clothes.

"I don't know," I said. "One second we were fighting and then I laughed when you fell, and it stopped."

"You think the snow stopped because I fell?"

"Actually, I know it sounds crazy, but I think it stopped because I laughed. The snow increased as we fought, so it would make sense that it stopped when we stopped fighting." As we spoke, the snow began to melt. "Look, as long as we aren't angry, the desert stays calm."

"Then I guess it's in both of our best interests if we stop fighting over stuff we can't control and work on getting to the next camp."

"I couldn't agree more."

As we continued our walk through the desert, the sun broke out, and soon, every trace of snow had vanished. The warm breeze dried our clothes as we walked, heating our once-shivering bodies. The sand turned hot, and I felt the heat in my boots that I had expected. We drank the water, and the heat turned us to puddles. By the time we reached the end, I missed the cool flurries.

I could see the camp ahead, and we headed straight for it, barely making our lunchtime deadline. An old woman hobbled from her tent as we approached.

"You two must be here about the Final Answer," she said.

"How did you know?" I asked.

"Oh, I have my ways. Come in, come in." She brought us into her home and offered us some food before retrieving a book from a nearby shelf.

"We have three clues so far, so this should be our fourth," I stated as we filled the old woman in on our journey.

"Well, this is an original copy of *Les Misérables* by Victor Hugo. I have a piece of a map marking the correct page."

Taking the book, I opened it and handed the map to Axen. "'Laughter is sunshine, it chases winter from the human face,'" I read.

Axen grunted. "Well, that one fits. It looks like this map gives us two options."

"Yes." The old woman pointed to the trails. "You can go through the enchanted village or around this volcano here. And I wouldn't wait too long to decide if you want to make it by dark."

***

ONCE UPON A BOOK

To go THROUGH THE ENCHANTED VILLAGE, *turn to page 201*
To go AROUND THE VOLCANO, *turn to page 207*

THROUGH THE MINE—THE
MAGICIAN'S NEPHEW

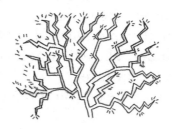

"I guess going down through the mine would give us better coverage." I looked at Axen as I finished up my meal. "Don't you think?"

"Yeah, that's probably best. Let's head in that direction."

I handed my plate to the old woman. "Before we go, is there anything else you can tell us about the Final Answer?"

"Only that you won't find the Final Answer written in a book. Only a descendent of the author who held it will be able to bring it forth."

"Why wouldn't the author have broken the brainwashing himself?" Axen asked.

"Oh, dear boy, by the time the author knew he held the key, the world was at a place with no hope. You cannot expect to hear the truth if you don't want to listen."

"How do we know people will listen now?" My eyebrows raised as I spoke.

"You're here, aren't you?" The old woman gestured to Axen and me, and we nodded. "It only takes one, my dear. And you, sir," she said to Axen, "had enough guts to find your way out. You will be all the hope this world needs."

"That's a lot to put on an ordinary guy's shoulders." Axen frowned.

"Ah, but you are not some ordinary guy. Now hurry along before it gets too late. I don't want you having to navigate after dark. Go on! And tell Aldred his old girlfriend said hello." She winked and then scurried back to her tent.

"Girlfriend?" I looked to Axen who shrugged. "Well, I guess we better be going." I thanked the rest of the campers, and Axen and I headed down a hill toward where the map showed the entrance to the mine.

Almost an hour of silence passed as we walked. Even the voices remained quiet. The afternoon stretched before us, and the warm sun hit my face.

"Axen, how much more do you think we need of the Final Answer?"

"I'm not sure, but something tells me we're close."

"How can you tell?"

Axen shrugged. "Again, I'm not sure. Something in my gut just feels like I know. It's as if I'm trying to remember something from my past. Do you know anything else about me and where I came from?"

"No, I'm sorry. I didn't know your family all that well. You tended to hang out with the older kids, and your sister was a little younger than me. I think maybe my younger sister might have played with her some. I don't even remember her name."

I saw the sadness sweep through Axen's eyes. "I ... I have a sister?"

My heart lurched. "Oh, Axen, I'm sorry. I didn't even think you might not remember her."

"No, it's okay." Axen blinked back tears. "I'm sure I'll remember one of these days. At least, I hope I do."

"Do you know anything about your life in Ashkelan?"

"No. Only that I was playing in the tower, and when I found the library, I picked up a book. That's it. Everything else is a blur."

"Not being able to remember your life must be terrible. Though, maybe not in some cases." I fought back my own tears.

"I take it you've been through something you'd like to forget?"

"Yes, but I'd rather not talk about it." Noticing a base of a hill up ahead, I pointed. "Look, there's the entrance to the mine."

Tucked in between some bushes, a wooden trap door was inlaid into the hill. An old key lay on the door with no lock in sight.

"I wonder what this is for." The rusted metal felt gritty against my fingers.

"Best to take it along until we find out," Axen responded.

I tucked it into my jacket, and we opened the trapdoor. A musty scent hit my nose as what smelled like decades worth of dusty air poured out. It was clear no one had been here in quite some time. Axen took a torch from his bag and lit it as we stepped onto the dark stairway that led down.

With him in the lead, I looked at the man-made walls of the shaft in the glow of the fire but should have paid more attention to my feet. My foot fell through one of the rotted steps, causing my ankle to twist in an unnatural way. Letting out a cry, I stumbled forward into Axen.

"Whoa!" He tripped but maintained his ground and helped me to my feet. "Are you okay?"

"Yes, I think so. Let's keep going." Hobbling on my foot, I kept moving.

It wasn't long before we reached a wider room with a door at one end and some electrical panels to the side.

"This must have been the control center. The miners would have turned the power on and off here, and the actual mine would be through that door," Axen explained and then turned to me. "Do you still have that key?"

"Yeah, it's right here." I reached inside my jacket but felt nothing but leather. "Well, it was. Where did it go?"

"I don't know but we better find it quick. This is my last torch and it's almost out."

"It must have fallen out when I tripped." I ran back toward the entrance, scanning the ground as I went. Axen joined me, but soon, the light of the torch grew dim.

"Maybe the electrical panel still works. Come on." Axen walked back to the panel. After a few moments of flicking switches and turning knobs, he sighed. "No luck." Our fire went out and we were left in pitch black. "Now what?"

"I don't know. Is there any way to jump the panel back to life?"

"It would need a jolt of high electricity to kick it back on." I heard Axen shuffle toward the panel. "And now that I think about it, I have the electricity that we need. Calessa, back away from the panel. This may make some sparks."

"What are you going to do?"

"I'm going to get angry."

My mind flashed back to the swamp. *He's going to let the shockwave run rampant again. That could kill him.* I was about to tell him to stop when I saw a flash of blue in the dark.

"Axen, please be careful!"

He gave no reply as I watched the lightning spread through his body, almost creating a glow around him. Sparks flew as he grabbed the main switch on the panel and forced it down with a yell of pain. The electricity left his body and ran through the system. The lights above us flickered and then turned bright as Axen collapsed to the ground.

I ran to his side. Sweat beading on his forehead, he breathed heavily. "Are you okay?"

"I'm fine. Find the key before this thing shuts down again." Running back to the entrance, I managed to find the key at the bottom of the stairs. Making it back to Axen, I unlocked the door and walked into the mine.

Mildewed boards lined the narrow corridor and rusty pickaxes littered the floor. This place had been left in a hurry, and I didn't want to know why. Blocking out the fears that jumped into my throat, I kept my eyes focused forward.

Thankfully, it didn't take long to make it through, and soon, we found the exit stairs that led back up to the top of the world. As we exited, I noticed the sun starting to set on the horizon, and up ahead stood a camp with a few disheveled-looking buildings.

We must not have looked threatening with Axen shuffling along and my limp because the members of the camp came out to greet us with looks of concern. After introductions and dinner, we all gathered around a fire.

"You two said you have four letters so far?" a woman asked.

"Yes," I said.

"Well, I know the author only left five clues. So, this must be your final one." She pulled a book from a bag and handed it to me. I read the cover aloud. "*The Magician's Nephew* by C. S. Lewis." My mind mulled over the name. "Why does that sound familiar?" I shook it off and opened the book to the marked page. "'No great wisdom can be reached without sacrifice.'" I looked to Axen. *He certainly sacrificed today.*

"So, where does that leave us?" Axen asked.

"I believe we have a W, a T, an I, an A, and now an N." I looked over to see the woman writing the letters down as I spoke. Handing me the piece of parchment, she looked at us.

"I think you better head on back to the base camp. The only one who may be able to decipher this is Aldred. He knows the authors of old better than any of us. But please, wait until morning to set out."

That night, I closed my eyes and wondered if tomorrow might be the day this would all end. What would I do then?

***

Turn to ENDING T *on page 213*

THROUGH THE RUINS—
FRANKENSTEIN

"Let's try the ruins," I said. "It may not be the safest, but I would love to see what some of the old world might have looked like."

"All right, then that's where we'll head," Axen said.

The old woman sat next to us. "Now remember, the Final Answer lies with a single author. I only know that there must be five clues to get you there."

"Well, we have four. So, as long as the next camp has our final one, we will be home free." Axen stood as he spoke.

"Yes, but what do we do once we have it?" I looked to the old woman for help.

"That I do not know, dear. All I can say is that the author's descendants will know the way. Now go on and get moving." She pulled me up and sent us on our way, calling out well wishes as we left.

Wandering over a hill, I let the voices chatter within. *I wonder who the descendant is. Maybe Aldred? He must be old enough to remember the authors. I wonder if Axen knows anything more about the Answers that could help.*

"Hey, Axen, how are we going to get back inside Ashkelan once we have the Final Answer?"

"I don't know. We may not have to. I'm not sure what it will take to break the brainwashing."

"Do you think we'll have to make it into their headquarters?"

"Possibly, but that would be almost impossible. That place is under tight security, and I'm sure now they know how we escaped through the wall they will be guarding that too."

"Well, can you think of anywhere that might be the heart of it all? I'm sure the answer will have to be said somewhere special."

"For all I know, we could say it right here and now and have it work. I am kind of hoping Aldred will know." Axen stopped for a moment and turned to me. "All I know for sure is we better pray we don't need to get inside those headquarters. It's not the kind of place you want to go back to once you've left." He turned back and continued walking.

"I know. I'm sorry for prying. I thought maybe you'd have something that could help."

"I wish I did. But besides taking my memories, the Answers stole my sense of being. Going back there would be like going back to a grave."

I chose to stay quiet as we neared the ruins. Great stone pillars stood in shambles, and half bits of wall crumbled as you passed. This wasn't just a building that had collapsed but an entire city. The voices in my mind filled in the missing details, and I could almost envision what this place must have looked like. Even in ruins, it seemed magnificent.

"I wonder what happened here," I said.

"Probably a result of the Answers."

"What do you mean?"

"The Answers attacked cities where they knew readers were hiding. This must have been one of them."

I could see the chaos that had ensued. Buildings lay in crumbles on the ground where they had been plowed down by force. Stones held scars of swordfights, and the air still felt thick with the stench of war. I turned to say something to Axen, but he looked to be in some sort of trance. His blue eyes had iced over, and he stared into nothingness.

"Axen, are you okay?" I got no response but saw emotions flicker through his eyes one by one—shock, then peace, then fear. It was as if he was seeing something in the invisible. Walking over to him, I shook his arm. "Axen, snap out of it!" A force emanated from him in a wavelength, pushing me back.

The shockwave pulsed around him like a mighty wind. I tried to yell to him but knew my voice would be lost in the roar. I watched as his eyes made more emotional turns. Sadness. Anger. And finally, defeat. The gust dissipated as fast as it began, and Axen crumpled to the ground.

"What just happened?" I asked.

"I just—"

Before Axen could finish, I heard a low rumble. A few pebbles fell on my arm, and I looked up. The ruins were beginning to shift. The ground began to shake, throwing me off balance. The repercussion of Axen's episode had caused an earthquake.

"Run!" I ran past Axen, grabbing his arm as I went.

Dodging the falling debris, we raced through the disintegrated city. The dust and debris coated us as we ran toward the edge of the city. We dove under a shaky archway as it buckled, barely escaping being crushed. Lying on the ground, I turned to Axen. We both had managed to get out with only a few scratches.

As we stood and dusted ourselves off, I looked ahead and saw the camp in the distance. It wouldn't be too much longer to reach it. Turning back, I asked again, "So what happened back there?"

Axen grabbed his head with his hand. "I saw the city before it was destroyed. It felt more like a memory than a vision. I think my family may have been from there." He winced. "I watched the Answers come in and destroy everything. They killed those who fought against them and took captives as they went. Then everything went dark as if the light in my mind shut off." Axen shook his head again and began walking toward the camp.

"So, I guess that's what caused the earthquake then—the shockwave that came off you."

"Most likely. I'm sorry if I hurt you."

"You didn't."

As we neared the camp, a few men and women came to greet us, and we filled them in on our story. Taking us back to their tents, they cleaned us up and gave us some dinner. Later, while sitting around the dinner table, a woman turned to speak to us.

"You two are close to the Final Answer."

"I know, we only need one more clue. We were hoping you had it," I said.

"Yes, dear, I know. But I also mean I believe you two are close in spirit to it. Somewhere in your hearts, I believe one of you already knows the answer you're looking for."

"You mean one of us might be the ancestor?" I asked.

"Anything is possible." The woman grabbed a book from a shelf nearby. "Here is your final clue. It's found in *Frankenstein* by Mary Shelley." She pushed the book across the table.

I pulled the book close and opened it. "'Nothing is so painful to the human mind as a great and sudden change,'" I read.

"So that gives us a W, a T, an I, an A, and an N." Axen trailed off in thought for a moment. "I think it's time we get back to Aldred. I think he'll have a better chance at this than us."

"Ah yes," the woman said. "Aldred knows the authors well. But please, leave in the morning. It's not safe to go by night."

***

Turn to ENDING T *on page 213*

THROUGH A LABYRINTH—GONE WITH THE WIND

"Let's try the labyrinth. I think we'll be able to navigate it," I said.

"I hope so. It would take too long to turn around and go another way if we can't." Axen turned to the campers. "Do you know anything else that may help us find the Final Answer?"

"You must follow your heart, my dear," the old woman said. "The answer is only one clue away. Find the final clue, figure out the author's name, and it will all become clear."

"Well, hopefully the next camp will have the final quote. I'm ready for this to come to an end." Axen stood and thanked our hosts and we set out across a hill.

"Axen, what do you think she meant by following your heart? Do you think she thinks you're the descendant that holds the answer?"

"I'm not sure. I don't even remember my own last name, so I'm not sure how I'm supposed to remember anything one of my ancestors said. I'm kind of hoping Aldred will know what to do."

"What will we have to do once we have the answer?"

"I guess we'll have to speak it over the people of Ashkelan. The only problem is where. And how to get back into the city is a problem all its own."

"I never thought about that. I doubt we'll get back in the way we came. Do you know of any other secret passages?"

"If I did, I wouldn't see it as a problem." Axen looked over his shoulder at me. "Maybe Aldred will have a fix for that too. He seems to know a lot about everything."

"That's true. Though, where do you think we'll have to go once we're inside the city?"

"I wish I didn't have to say it, but my best guess would be Answers Headquarters."

"What's it like there?" I tried to keep up with Axen's long strides.

"Empty."

"But how? Wouldn't that place be swarming with people?"

"Well, yes. There are multiple labs, bunkrooms, eateries, and more. But the whole place feels like an empty space. No one cares about you there. They don't care who you are or where you came from. You're only a number to them. Another drone to brainwash and manipulate. There's no learning there. Nothing new, just the same thought processes built by some idiotic scientists hundreds of years ago."

"I never thought about it like that. I can't imagine not being able to read again. It's almost like it's a part of me now that I know I can."

"Well, it is. Humans were never meant to be held back. The Answers had no right to do what they did. But fear can make people do crazy things. I'm glad I got out when I did. The next step for me would have made it much harder to get away."

"What do you mean?"

"My next session would have been my final one. Once they complete that, you become a worker for the Answers. I would have been stationed in the very tower I was taken from. I would have been in charge of gathering new readers as they came."

"So, you would have been who I was running from back in the library." My mind tried to wrap around what would have happened if I'd been caught.

"Yes." Axen stopped for a moment. "But that didn't happen. I think we should be focusing on what's ahead of us rather than behind." He started walking again.

I let the warmth of the afternoon sun wash over me as I walked. The trek up the hill was an easy one, and soon I could see the labyrinth in the distance. Hedges, wood, trees, and stones made the walls of the maze, and even looking down on it, a direct path through seemed difficult to comprehend. As we drew closer, the walls seemed to grow higher and higher. By time we reached the entrance, they were twice as tall as Axen. There wouldn't be any room for cheating our way through this puzzle.

I pointed to a large sign off to the side. "There's a sign." Walking over, I read, "'Don't be fooled by pictures and signs. Trust the voice within your mind.' I have a feeling this isn't going to be as easy as we had hoped."

Stepping beneath a vined archway, I looked at the maze stretched out before me. At least five passages could be seen from the beginning, and each had signs above them. Two had green markings, and the other three held a yellow and two red.

"I'm guessing we should start at a green path?" I asked.

"I think that's a fair guess." Axen started in toward the first path.

Walking behind him, I reached out to feel the cool leaves of the hedges that made the walls. Running my fingers against the greenery as I walked, I noticed an odd sensation. Turning to look, the leaves had enveloped my hand and thin vines were crawling up my arm. I let out a shriek and tried to pull away.

Axen turned to look and then began to search his bag. "Calessa, catch!"

He tossed me a small knife from his pack. I caught the blade with my free hand and cut the vines from my arm. The leaves shriveled back into the hedge, and I turned to Axen.

"I don't think this is the right way." I turned back toward the entrance. "We need to go back."

"What other path do you want to take? If the green one tried to kill you, what do you expect from the red or yellow?"

Axen had a point, and we continued, though I was careful not to touch the walls as I went. Reaching the end of the corridor, we came to a fork in our path. Signs hung over the archways at each entrance. To the right lay a stone path, and the left held a tree-lined trail.

"Which way?" I asked.

"They both have green markings. I think we should go this way." Axen headed into the stone road and I followed warily. Something didn't seem right about this maze. Walking along, I noticed etchings in the stone. Looking closer, I saw that they were names and titles of books I had never heard of. My eyes lit up with eagerness at all the stories I had yet to read, and I drank in the words as we went. We reached the end of the road, and a wider expanse stretched out with three options for our next path.

These three weren't marked with colors but, rather, had an X, an arrow, and cloud drawn on wooden signs at the entrances. Axen headed for the arrow, which was a trail that led straight into a cave, but something about the large X drew me in. Wandering over to the sign, I saw someone had carved something at the bottom.

"Axen, this sign has a note." I heard him sigh as he trudged my way. "It says, 'Go this way.'"

"Calessa, I keep telling you, nothing good ever comes from an X or any other warning sign."

I stood my ground. "If you want to go that way, fine. I'll be here when you get back. The entrance said to trust the voice, and mine is telling me we need to go this way."

"Fine. But you're wasting our time."

Axen walked into the cavern and I waited in silence. A few moments later, I heard a loud crash, and a flash of light emitted from the hole. A moment later, Axen emerged, his hair in disarray and his face covered in soot. I wasn't sure I wanted to know.

Walking past me without a word, he entered the X-marked trail. I swallowed a snicker and went after him. Reaching the next choice, we checked the signs and found there was another with small etchings telling us which way was safe. Following the words the previous readers left behind, we made it out of the labyrinth with little trouble.

As we exited, I could see the camp not too far off. The sun painted the sky as it set, and the warm air clung in the dusk. A group of men and women greeted us as we reached the camp.

"Hello," a woman said. "Aren't you two quite a sight. Well, at least you are." She looked at Axen's smoky face.

After a quick round of introductions, Axen was led off to get cleaned up, and the woman invited me to come help her prepare for dinner.

"Do you have a final clue for us?" I asked as I chopped some vegetables.

"We do, and I believe you two will need to find your way back to the base camp quickly. This world is getting worse by the minute. I'm hoping you will save us all."

"That's a lot of responsibility."

"Ah, yes. But I have faith in you. Now come along, it's time to eat."

After dinner, the woman handed us a book. I glanced at the cover. *Gone with the Wind* by Margaret Mitchell. I opened it and read the underlined quote. "'Now you are beginning to think for yourself instead of letting others think for you. That's the beginning of wisdom.'"

"That puts us at five," Axen said. "W, T, I, A, and N." I could almost see the gears turning in his mind. "We need to get to Aldred."

***

Turn to ENDING T *on page 213*

THROUGH THE BOG—THE LITTLE PRINCE

"I guess the bog. I don't know if I'm up for navigating an entire labyrinth. Not after being drug around by non-goblin troll creatures all morning." I stood up as I spoke.

"Before you leave, I think you should know that you two are close to the Final Answer." The old woman spoke gently. "I believe within the day you will have your final clue. Then you must hurry back to Aldred. He will know the author the clues lead to."

"We will." Axen grabbed his pack. "Thank you for your wisdom and hospitality, but I think it's time we head out. I want to make it to the next camp by nightfall."

Heading out toward a hill in the distance, I pressed for more information about Axen's time with the Answers.

"So, how many new members get inducted each year?" I asked.

"The number gets higher each year, it seems. When I was inducted, they only found about three to four kids a year that could read. But now this past year, that number has almost doubled. Something must have shifted to allow more kids to be able to read. Either that or the Answers made the library easier to find so more kids would find their way there."

"Why wouldn't the Answers test kids as they reach a certain age or something to see if they can read? Why make it so private?"

"My best guess is that they don't want an uprising. They also know that any smart person—and most readers are fairly smart—would try to trick the system and pretend they can't read to fool them."

"So that's why they have the library. No one is going to try to hide their surprise if they think they're alone."

"Exactly. I often tried to get out long enough to spread the word about it so that maybe the kids would stop playing in the tower, but I knew once I got out, there was no going back in. If I had escaped into the city, I would have been an easy target, and you don't want to know what they do to a fugitive once they're caught."

I caught Axen's arm, causing him to stop. "Now you have to tell me."

He turned to look at me, and I saw the pain in his eyes.

"They use them as prototypes for new therapy techniques, torturing them mercilessly until they either die or become so brainwashed they can't live on their own." Axen shook off my hold and continued walking.

I scrambled to catch up. "What do they do with them if they reach that point?"

"There's a ward in the basement of the headquarters where they send all the 'drones' as they call them. They're mindless robots at that point and need caregivers to care for them. If they wouldn't have that, they'd waste away within a matter of days."

"That's terrible. I'm a little surprised the Answers keep them around, though. I would have thought they'd find a way to get rid of them."

"Well, they have been working on a serum that has the potential to bring back some of their ability. Their minds would still be gone, but their strength would increase."

I stopped for a moment, my eyes growing wide. "They're building an army," I murmured.

"Yeah, and a nasty one at that," Axen called over his shoulder. "But hopefully by tomorrow, we won't need to worry about that. Speaking of which, there's the bog."

I looked down the hill and saw a foggy expanse stretching out over a few miles. I watched the warm afternoon sun grow dim as we trekked down the hill. Damp tendrils of air drifted around me, sending chills down my spine. *This is not going to be a pleasant trip.*

The voices continued to gripe as we neared the bog. My boots sunk with each step, and I could feel the pull of the ground as if it wanted to swallow me whole.

"How do you expect us to get through this?" Axen complained. "We should have gone to the labyrinth. At least that was probably solid ground." His boots made squishing sounds as he walked.

"Oh, I'm sure it won't be that bad." I ignored my own inner voices as they continued to scream their displeasure. "You would have been just as grumpy if we had gone to the maze. At least here, we don't have to try to solve anything. It's a straight shot to the next camp."

"Yeah, a straight shot through a swamp."

I continued and I soon felt the mud splash my legs as I entered the marshy waters. Sloshing through, I looked at the scraggly trees filling the area. Slimy vines hung in such density that it made it hard to see. Moving them to the side, I pressed on. It wasn't the ideal journey, but so far it beat some of the other challenges we had faced.

"This was a terrible idea. Why couldn't we have gone around this place?" Axen continued to mumble under his breath, and I tried to hold back a snicker. It seemed as if no matter where we went, Axen wasn't too happy about it.

"Can't you ever find the good in something?"

"What good?" he yelled, despite being only two feet from me. "This whole world has been destroyed. Ashkelan is about to be destroyed, and we still haven't found the answer." I saw a flicker of light go through his eyes as his anger flared. "I escaped the Answers to find a better life and what did I get? A week's worth of near-death experiences with a chatterbox who doesn't know anything."

"Axen!"

He stopped mid-rant and looked at me. "What?"

"Look." I pointed to his feet. The heat from the electricity running within him had caused him to sink deeper into the mud.

I watched his eyes turn from anger to concern as he tried to move. "Help me get out of here." His tone was still red hot.

"You need to calm down."

"I *am* calm."

I could see the mud creeping higher as a layer of steam rose off his skin.

"Sure, you are." He sensed my tone and glared. "Look, if you don't calm down, you're going to sink further."

Axen tried to force his way out, struggling against the pull of the bog.

"Trying to fight it isn't helping either!" I made my way over to him and laid my hand on his hot arm. "You need to cool off."

"And how do you suggest I do that?" His teeth clenched.

"Well, first off, relax your jaw." He did. "Now try to think about something besides the trouble you're in. Look, you may see this world as a mess, and you have every right to, but in my eyes, this world is a miracle. Think about it! All this time, an entire world had been thriving right outside our walls. To me, even this bog is better than being holed up in Ashkelan. Can't you see that everything is okay if you're free?"

I saw the mud begin to recede from his boots, and Axen cooled to the touch.

"I guess you have a point."

He took a deep breath and moved his leg forward. After a few more deep breaths, Axen was able to move freely, and we continued our way through the grime. Reaching the end of the marsh, I could see the next camp off through the haze.

"Do you think they'll let us walk straight into the camp?" I asked.

"Well, I don't see how we could look too threatening covered in vines and mud. Our only concern is if they think we're some kind of monsters."

Axen led the way toward the camp, and I soon saw we had nothing to worry about. A woman came from a group of people to meet us near the edge of a line of tents.

"What happened? Are you two all right?" she asked.

"Yes, we're fine. Just a little misadventure through a bog. Looks like we went the messy way to get here."

I tried to keep it lighthearted as we made introductions and filled the woman in on our journey. She listened intently and invited us into the camp. Sitting around a fire, we watched as she went to get our final clue. I caught a glimpse of the cover as she passed. *The Little Prince* by Antoine de Saint-Exupéry.

"This was my ancestor's and I believe it holds your final clue." The woman opened the book and read. "'No one is ever satisfied where he is.'"

I glanced at Axen and saw him duck his head. Choosing not to bring attention to the obvious, I thought through the clues we had received so far.

"A W, a T, an I, an A, and an N." I looked to Axen. "Any ideas?" He shook his head but said nothing.

"I wish I was better versed in the authors of old," the woman said. "But alas, I think your best choice will be to get to Aldred as quickly as you can. He should be able to help. Though I think you two have had enough adventure for one day. You can leave in the morning."

***

Turn to ENDING T *on page 213*

THROUGH THE MANSION—
SHERLOCK HOLMES

"I'm curious what the old mansion looks like," I said.

"Then let's go that way." Axen looked at the old woman. "Do you have any more information about the Final Answer before we head out?"

"Only that there are five clues that lead to the author's name. If you're lucky, this next camp will have the final one." The woman took my hand and led me to the side. "Now, dear, I have something important to tell you," she whispered.

"Yes, what is it?"

The woman glanced at Axen as he studied the map. "Don't let that one go. He's a keeper."

I smiled. "Yes, ma'am. I don't intend to."

"Good, if only I had listened to my own advice, perhaps Aldred and I would still be together." She hobbled off, leaving me slack-jawed.

I walked back to Axen as he picked up his bag.

"Time to go," he said. "I want to reach the next camp before dark."

We thanked our host and headed out the door and toward a hill in the distance.

"What did the old woman want to tell you?" Axen asked.

"Oh, nothing." I grabbed his hand. "Just some grandmotherly advice."

"Uh-uh, and why are you smiling like a crazy person?"

"No reason. So, what do you think we'll have to do once we find the Final Answer?"

"I'm not sure, but my best bet will be that whoever the ancestor of the author is will have it, so we'll have to track them down. Then I'm guessing we'll have to sneak back into Ashkelan."

"Do you know how to do that?"

"Not at all. The only way I knew of to get in and out was that tunnel inside the wall. I don't even know where we'll have to go once we're in. Probably headquarters."

"What is headquarters like?" I asked.

"Boring." Axen chuckled. "I'm sure it's must more interesting if you buy in to all the Answers' beliefs. But for someone looking in from the outside, it looks like a building full of mindless minions. No one talks to you, and you never learn anything new. They implant thoughts into your brain and hope they stick."

"Sounds horrible."

"It is. I was hoping never to go back, but I guess that's the price of trying to be the hero." Axen smirked.

"I don't know about heroes. We're ordinary people."

"Trust me, if we can help even a few of those who were conscripted, we'll be heroes. The Answers have destroyed so many lives. I just hope to be able to save the people of Ashkelan any more heartbreak."

"Do you think the Answers will ever stop brainwashing people?" I asked.

"Never. If it was in their power, they probably would have

the whole city brainwashed by now. The original scientists went too far, and the minions that took their place become more deluded every day. They're emotionless and have no recollection of what it means to be humane. The process is getting more and more traumatizing, and they don't even know to care."

I could tell Axen was getting heated as a flash of electricity blitzed through his eyes.

"Well, I'm sure we'll find the answer soon and then this will all be over."

I squeezed his hand and tried to calm his anger as we reached the top of the hill. I could see the mansion in the distance. Three stories high, the building loomed over the surrounding land. The old stone was starting to lose a battle against the moss which almost covered the mansion from foundation to chimney. The windows had been shattered, and the grounds around it looked almost as broken. Weed-encased walkways led to the door and around the building. The grass, yellowed and dead, withered in the slight breeze. The only sign of life was the garden which seemed almost as beautiful and expansive as the mansion itself.

I started to head toward the colorful growth when I felt a pull from Axen back toward the main entrance of the house. I reached to knock on the front door, but Axen opened it before I could.

"I doubt anyone's home." He smirked as he stepped inside. The inner rooms looked much more luxurious than the outside suggested. Spotless porcelain floors stretched through the grand foyer. Elaborate plants and pieces of art filled every wall, and a grand staircase spiraled up from the center of the room.

"This reminds me of the place on the lake," I said as I gaped at the wondrous surroundings.

Axen walked over to what looked like a switch on the wall. "I'm assuming this controls the chandelier." He flipped the switch, but nothing happened. He flicked it up and down a few more times, but not the slightest bit of light escaped the crystal masterpiece above.

"Maybe it's broken?"

"I guess so," Axen said, returning to the center of the floor.

"Which way should we go to get through to the back?" I asked.

"Well, there's no door straight back, so I guess we'll have to find our way through the other rooms. Let's go this way."

Walking to the nearest door, Axen reached for the knob but missed. My mind did a double take, and I watched as he tried again. Finally, he reached once more, and his fingers smashed into a wall.

"The door's been painted on," I exclaimed. "How odd. Let's try the next one." I reached to open the second door and it opened with ease. Swinging it wide, my mouth fell open as I came face to face with a solid brick wall.

"I think maybe we'll have to go around the outside," Axen said as he started to head back to the door.

"Wait. Let's try the stairs."

I tested the stairs validity and found them as solid as the floor. I climbed one by one, keeping an eye on each footing to make sure I wouldn't fall through.

"Calessa, you're not going anywhere," Axen said.

"What do you mean I'm—" I looked up to see that while I had taken at least twenty-five steps, I was no closer to the second floor than when I began. Dumbfounded, I turned back and stepped down to the main floor. Axen walked to the front door and pulled on the handle.

"It's locked." He turned to me. "We're trapped."

"Nothing is as it seems." I pondered this for a moment, and then an idea struck me. "Axen, if the doors are fake and the staircase doesn't climb, then maybe something we wouldn't consider a door is the way out."

"What do you mean?"

"I have an idea. Follow me." I raced to the back of the room where a large picture window looked out at what had been a beautiful courtyard in its time. I pushed against the side of the window and found my idea had been right—the window was the door. Two of the huge panes swung open, revealing a path out into the sun. I glanced back at Axen before walking through. He followed, and we closed the glass door behind us.

"How did you know what to do?" he asked.

"I don't know. I just decided to ignore what I thought was practical. Nothing about this journey has been normal anyway."

Axen shrugged, and we started through the courtyard. When we reached the other side, I could see the camp not too far off. We made quick work of the rest of the trip, and soon, were being greeted by a group of men and women from the camp.

"Who are you two?" a woman asked.

"I'm Calessa, and this is Axen. We've come from the base camp."

It didn't take much more than that for the campers to warm up to us. Soon, we were seated around a fire talking about our journey and how far we'd come.

"We have your final clue for you," the woman said, handing us a book. I looked at the cover: *Sherlock Holmes* by Arthur Conan Doyle. I opened it to read a quote that had been underlined.

"'There is nothing more deceptive than an obvious fact.'" I looked to Axen. "That leaves us with a W, an S, an I, an F, and now a T. Those letters mean anything to you?"

"No, but I bet they will to Aldred." Axen put his arm around me as we snuggled close in the cool air. "But I think it would be in our best interest if we stayed here for the night. We'll head out in the morning."

***

Go to ENDING S *on page 219*

THROUGH THE GARDEN—A MIDSUMMER'S NIGHT DREAM

"I think we should go through the garden. I'm not sure I'm comfortable going through someone's home," I said.

"Well, dear, I'll let you know that whoever lived there is long gone." The old woman stood nearby as Axen and I looked at the map. "And as for the Final Answer, you should know there are only five clues that lead to the author that knows it."

"Well then, we only have one more to go," Axen said.

"You two better be on your way. I wouldn't want you to have to travel at night," the old woman said. "And be sure to give Aldred my hello. I miss that old geezer."

"We will." I smiled and thanked her before turning to Axen. "You ready to go?"

Axen nodded, and we headed toward a hill nearby. My skin felt warm from the sun, and I breathed in the fresh air. Grabbing Axen's hand, I settled in for a what I hoped to be a peaceful afternoon.

"So, do you have family back in Ashkelan? If you do, I'd love to meet them," Axen said.

So much for peaceful. The one subject I tried to avoid.

"Uh, not really. I have a sister, but I think you've already met her."

"If I did, I don't remember. How would I have known her?"

"I think she used to play with your sister back before you disappeared."

Axen stopped and his eyes flickered. "I had a sister. I had forgotten all about her." He looked at me. "What happened to my family after I left?"

"I don't really know. They kind of secluded themselves after you were gone. Your parents seemed to keep your sister pretty close to them, and we never saw them out and about."

"They must think I'm dead by this point."

"I think a lot of the families that lost someone to the Answers think that. Until you told me, I assumed they were killed for trespassing on Answer property."

"Trust me, that would have been much more humane than the truth. The Answers have become monsters. Obviously, the original scientists have passed away, and minions have taken their place. Every few generations, new minions take over as the old die off, and each new set of leaders has been more brainwashed than the last. At this point, the leaders are heartless and all but brainless. They come up with new therapies every few months that are more traumatizing than the previous ones. To be honest, I think they may be building an army."

"What for?" I asked. "Nothing has threatened them that I know of."

"They're afraid. That's been the one common thread through all the leaders tracing back to the original core. They're afraid of anything they can't control, so they're planning to control everything."

"So, they plan to attack the city?"

"I think so. That's why we need to find this answer, and now. I just hope we're in time."

"That's if we can find the descendant of the author." I looked over the hill as we reached the top and saw our destination. A large mansion stood alone on a plot of land.

FAITH WEAVER

The shingles falling from the roof and the vines crawling up the stone made it obvious no one had been here in quite some time. The cracked walkways and dead grass made for an ugly sight. I was shocked at the state of the garden, however, to the right of the mansion.

"It's beautiful." My voice came out thinner than a breath.

The large garden stretched even farther than the mansion and, unlike the building, was in near perfect condition. Colorful flowers filled the area and a thin trail led through the midst of the beauty.

As we neared, I saw butterflies of all sizes flittering their way from bloom to bloom. The aromatic air seemed almost too sweet to inhale but felt intoxicating at the same time. I wandered onto the cobblestone path, letting my fingers drag along the different textures of each flower.

"I wonder how this place has stayed so nice," I said.

"I don't know. Who would bother with the garden but leave the house to fall apart?"

I looked closer at the petals of a soft rose. A slight glimmer shone off the flower as if it had been dusted with a fine glitter.

"Axen, do you notice anything strange about the plants? It almost as if they're magical or something." I noticed Axen wiping his hands on his pants—now coated with a shimmery substance. I snickered as I watched him spread it further in an attempt to brush it off.

"They're sparkly, that's for sure," he grumbled.

"I wonder what could cause something like this. Do you remember reading anything about glittery plants back at headquarters?"

"Not that I know of. I'm starting to think maybe there's some other force at work here." Axen stood in the center of the garden, trying to avoid anything that might add to his shiny new outfit.

"I wonder who did this."

"I did! And if you don't leave now, I'll tear you limb from limb!"

I jumped at the sound of a small voice from behind me. I turned but didn't see anyone.

"Who's there?"

"Down here, you giant! I told you, get out before I get even more angry."

I looked down and noticed something standing on the petal of a daisy. Kneeling, I came face to face with an angry being. A tiny nose poked out from a stubborn face. The little being stood no taller than my finger and had iridescent wings extending from her petite frame.

"What are you?" I asked.

Her tiny ears turned red.

Axen came to my side. "She's a fairy."

"I prefer the term pixie." Her needle thin arms stood out as she put her hands on her hips with defiance. "Now get out of here before I take you both to the ground!"

I chuckled. "I'm sorry to offend you, but I don't think you'd have much luck."

My words seemed to have tipped her over her little edge, because soon she flew up and pulled at my dark hair.

"Hey!" I yelled and stood.

"Get off her!"

Axen tried to swat at the sprite as she circled our heads at a dizzying pace. She dove at Axen's face, causing him to lose his balance and fall flailing into a group of wildflowers.

"See! Told you, I could take you the ground," the pixie sneered.

I held back a chuckle as Axen stood, covered from head to toe in shimmering particles.

I turned back to the sprite. "Look, Pixie. I'm sorry we came into your garden, but I promise we mean no harm. We're trying to get through so we can be on our way. Will you please let us pass?"

The fairy stopped and hovered in front of my nose, making me almost go cross-eyed looking at her. "And why should I do that?"

"Well, why do you care about the garden?" I countered.

"Because it's always been my home." She backed away and then sat on a leaf. "I was happy when all the other pixies of the realm came here to play, but now, there is no realm left, and I'm the only one." Her tiny face took on a pout.

"Well, look ... if you let us go, we're going to try to restore the realms. If we can, maybe the other fairies, sorry, I mean pixies, will come back. Sound like a deal?"

She huffed as loudly as she could and stood. "Fine! But don't come back here if you can't bring my friends!"

Before I could say another word, she flittered off behind a bush, and Axen and I were left to navigate the garden alone. When we reached the end, we could see the camp in the distance.

"I hope they have something to clean you up," I joked as we walked. "I'm not sure sparkle is a good color on you."

"Oh, hush." Axen scowled as we walked, and soon we reached the camp.

A woman came out to meet us and invited us in for dinner but only if Axen agreed to wash his hands first.

After eating, we gathered around a fire. The woman brought a book out to Axen and me. *A Midsummer's Night Dream* by William Shakespeare. I opened the book to a marked page and laughed. I looked at Axen as I read. "'Though she be but little, she is fierce.'"

Axen snorted. "You can say that again."

The woman looked at us with curious eyes but asked no questions. I thought for a moment before looking to Axen again.

"So, we have all five clues. W, S, I, F, and T. I wonder what it means."

"Aldred will know," the woman spoke up. "You must hurry to him. The descendant will know the answer. But for now, I think you two should rest. You have a long day ahead of you tomorrow."

***

Go to ENDING S *on page S*

THROUGH THE GHOST TOWN—
TREASURE ISLAND

"I'd like to see the abandoned town if that's okay," I said.

"Works for me." Axen looked at the old woman. "Any more advice or information you might have for us?"

"There are five clues to the author's identity and only a descendant of said author will know the Final Answer. Other than that, I'll leave you with one piece of grandmotherly advice. You two would make an adorable couple!" The old woman snatched the book and headed back to her tent, leaving Axen and I to sit in shock, red-faced.

Choosing not to say anything to make the awkward situation worse, we thanked the members of the camp and left. Walking toward a hill, I tried to steer the conversation clear of the old woman's crazy notion.

"So, what do think we'll have to do with the Final Answer once we get it?" I asked.

"I don't know for sure. Something tells me we'll have to sneak back into headquarters. I was hoping not to have to go back. I guess that was too good to be true."

"Well, at least when we go back, we'll know our way in, right?"

"No. They'll have that tunnel guarded well now that they know we escaped. We'll have to find another entrance."

"You knew when you left you'd be sealing off your only known entrance back into the city?"

"Yeah. I figured once I got out, I wouldn't have to go back. I would have been out even earlier if it hadn't been for you."

"Me? What did I have to do with it?" I stopped Axen and turned him to look at me.

"Well, if you hadn't been so cute and helpless just standing there, I wouldn't have had to stop. I couldn't just leave you there." He turned bright red and then continued up the hill.

"Well, excuse me for being oblivious." I smirked as I tried to match his pace.

"Uh-huh. I don't think you're that sorry." He turned and looked into me with those electric eyes.

"You're right. I'm not sorry at all. But why did you wait this long to tell me how you felt? Would've been nice to know you felt differently."

"Well, once you're conscripted into the Answers, they try to strip all emotion from you. Emotions lead to brash decisions. Kind of like this one." Axen leaned in and gave me a quick kiss before turning and walking away.

My mind blanked, and I almost remembered what it was like before the voices. My fingers grazed my lips where they tingled from the electric shock that had jolted through me when we kissed. Lost in a daze, I was only snapped out of it by Axen calling from up ahead.

"Calessa! Come on, I wouldn't have done that if I thought it would turn you to stone."

I was about to retort his insult when I saw a glimmer of mischief in his eye. Rushing to the top of the hill where he stood, I playfully punched his arm.

"You have no idea what you're getting yourself into," I said.

"I'm the one who's been brainwashed. I think I can handle a spunky little moxie." Axen held out his hand, and I let mine glide between his calloused fingers.

Looking down over the hill, I could see the abandoned town splayed out in front of me. The smell of rotting wood mixed with the fresh breeze reached my nose as we wandered down to the village.

"I wonder how long it's been since anyone's lived here," I said.

"Probably before Ashkelan was built, if I had to guess." Axen let go of my hand and sauntered into the town square like he owned the place.

The buildings looked as if a harsh breath could knock them down with ease. I had never seen so much trash and debris. Glass bottles, papers, and broken wood lay strewn in every corner. Signs hung above some of the structures indicating what businesses used to fill the space. A bank, a hotel, and a library were among the few left standing. I gravitated toward the library, but Axen caught my arm before I could climb the steps to the entrance.

"You're not going to want to go in there. That roof could collapse at any minute."

Books were scattered everywhere on the ground surrounding the building. Most had pages torn out or looked as if they had been burned, but that didn't stop me from picking one up and beginning to read.

"Aha! I knew you twos were readers!"

I dropped the book and spun around. A man older than Aldred hobbled his way out from the hotel across the street.

"Who are you?" I asked.

"Doesn't matter! What matters is that I got myself two readers here who can save my life. Now you two come with me." He used a bony finger to beckon us closer to the hotel, and Axen and I followed with tentative steps. As we entered the building, I saw stacks of papers and books filling every inch of the main room.

"Sir, are you alright? Do you need some kind of help?" Axen asked.

The man spun around and looked at us with wild eyes. "Yes, I do, sonny! I need ya'll to write me a better story. That must be the only way to get out of this mess!"

"What do you mean?" I asked. "You want us to write something? I don't even know how."

"Sure, you do! You twos are readers, aren't ya?" The man's spindly finger pointed at us.

"Well yes, but aren't you a reader too?" I inched closer to Axen.

"Nope, never learned how. Now, I keep trying to figure it out on these darn books, and all I want is to get out of here."

"I think he's crazy," Axen whispered to me.

"Be nice," I whispered back. "It's clear he's been through a lot."

"Would you two stop your whisperings and help me already?" The man scrambled to bring us some scraps of parchment and a pencil each.

"Sir, I'm sorry, but I don't understand. I can't write you anything." I tried to stay calm.

"Liar!" he yelled. "If you two won't write, then you must be the Answers come to take me away!"

"No, we aren't. I promise. Please, calm down." I tried to approach the man, but he scurried behind a stack of books.

"You two must be here to kill me! That's it! You'll never take me alive!" The old man emerged from the stack, holding a small wooden knife in his hands.

"That's not what we said! Why won't you believe us?" Panic set in as I backed up to where was Axen stood.

"Now, calm down, sir," Axen said, stepping in front of me. "Calessa, I want you to run," he whispered back to me.

"No, I'm not leaving you!"

"I'll be right behind you." He pushed me toward the door.

The old man began to rage. Incoherent shouts tumbled from his mouth and he waved the blade in Axen's face. I turned and bolted out the door. As I ran down the street, I looked back to see Axen racing behind me, the old man left standing on the front stoop, screaming after us. Reaching the edge of town, I stopped to catch my breath. Axen caught up, and I saw he held the wooden knife.

"He wasn't hard to disarm," Axen said with a chuckle. "Poor guy must have been here a while. He was long gone in the mental department."

I turned back to the path and saw the camp not too far off.

"I wonder why he never went to the camp," I said.

"I'm not sure. Not much we can do about it now."

Axen reached for my hand, and we headed toward the group of men and women I could see in the distance. A woman came to greet us outside the camp lines as we neared. After introductions and filling her in on our journey, we followed the woman back to her tent.

"Here is your final clue," she said, handing me a book.

"Treasure Island by Robert Lewis Stevenson." I read. Opening to a marked page, I found the quote. "'Sir, with no intention to take offense, I deny your right to put words in my mouth.'"

"So that leaves us with a W, a T, an I, an F, and an S." Axen rattled off our clues.

"The Final Answer will not be a written clue like you have had so far. Aldred will know what to do. You must get to him quickly," the woman said.

***

Go to ENDING S *on page 219*

THROUGH THE WOODS—THE ADVENTURES OF HUCKLEBERRY FINN

"The woods will give you the best coverage," the old woman said.

"That sounds like a good idea. After this morning, I'm not sure I'd want to risk running into any more former Answers who may be hiding in that abandoned town. No offense." Axen stood as he spoke, nodding to the man from the jungle.

"None taken," the man replied.

"Do you have anything else we may need to know before we leave?" I looked to the old woman.

"There is only one clue left for you to find. After that, you will need to find the heart of the Answers and speak the Final Answer there."

"Where's the heart, then?" I asked.

"I do not know." The old woman shook her head. "But you two better be on your way. I don't want you traveling in the dark."

Axen and I gathered our things and headed toward a hill in the distance. I felt the heat radiate off my skin in the afternoon sun, the sweat forming on my brow.

"What do you think she meant by the heart of the Answers?" I asked.

"I don't know. Maybe somewhere in headquarters?"

"Well, how would we get there?"

"I don't know that either." Axen looked back at me. "I only knew of the one way in and out, and now that I used it to escape, I doubt they'll leave it unguarded."

"Well, is there a certain place inside the headquarters that would be at the center or something?"

"Not that I can think of, though I'm not sure they mean the heart as in a literal location, but more like the soul of the organization. Not that anybody in the Answers even has a soul anymore."

"You mean the brainwashing is that bad?"

"You have no idea. The electromagnetic therapy is more painful than anything I have ever experienced. They not only try to take your memories, but, sadly, they also try to drain your will to be anyone but their minion."

"Axen, I'm so sorry." I reached out and put my hand on his arm, and he leaned into it. *Am I crazy or did he just lean into me?* I shushed the voices and kept my focus ahead. Looking over the hill as we reached the top, I could see the forest below. Dense and dark, the trees towered above the ground.

"That looks much creepier than the other forests we've seen," I said.

"Yeah, it doesn't look inviting, but I'm sure we'll be all right." Axen reached back and took my hand. "Let's go."

My jaw went slack as I let Axen lead me down the hill. *I wonder if he knows what he just did.* Before the voices could say anything else, I got my answer. Axen let go of my hand, and I saw his neck turn red as he continued toward the forest.

The bark of the trees was all but black, and the leaves were the darkest green I had ever seen. Something felt odd in the air here. The thick breeze breathed down my neck, coating me in an eerie chill.

"You ready?" Axen asked, suddenly at my side.

"I suppose," I said.

My vision left me as I stepped into the shadows. Screaming, I backed out of the trees where I tripped over a root and fell right into Axen's arms. I looked up into his stormy eyes as he caught me for the second time in the past two days.

"Are you okay?"

"Uh ... um. The forest. It makes you blind," I stammered as I tried to regain my footing.

Axen helped me to my feet and walked over to the woods. I watched as he took a step in and immediately jumped back.

"How are we supposed to get through now?" I asked.

"I have no idea. But there has to be a way." Axen began walking along the edge of the forest, sticking his head in every so often and pulling back quickly.

I stepped back in, hoping my eyes would adjust to the pitch black. After several minutes, I backed out carefully. Only this time, the sun didn't flood my eyes like it had the first time. I still couldn't see.

"Axen!" I yelled, reaching frantically around me. "I can't see anything. Don't stay in the shadows." I felt around, and soon my hand hit Axen's chest as he pulled me into him.

"Don't worry, I'm here," he whispered as he held me close. My heart raced, and the voices in my mind spilled out my mouth.

"Axen, I can't see. What do I do? Can you see? How can I—"

Axen pressed his lips to mine. A moment later, he pulled back, and I stammered.

"Still blind?" Axen asked, still holding me against his chest.

"Yes ... But I think things are starting to come back into focus."

"I think the longer you stay in the shadows, the longer it takes for your vision to return."

"Then how are we supposed it make it through?" I asked, pulling back to look at Axen, my vision clearing away like a morning fog.

"See those spots of sunlight in the forest?" Axen pointed at small patches of light scattered throughout the woods. Some were only inches apart while others were much larger.

"Are you saying we have to stay in the sunlight?"

"I think that might be the only way. However, it will be slow going if we have to let our sight return at any point. So, we need to move quickly."

"Okay," I sighed. "Let's go." Stepping over a shadow into the first patch of light, I looked around. Our suspicions were solidified: my sight remained intact as long as I stood in the sun. We were forced to travel through a small shadow onto the next patch and had to wait a moment after for our vision to clear. Hours later, it looked as if we still had quite a way to go.

"Axen, what are we going to do when the sun goes down?"

He stopped and looked up. Dusk was already descending. The oranges and reds stretched as far as we could see, making our patches of light a little dimmer.

"I think we're going to have to start moving quicker and not waiting as long between movements."

"But how? We'll be blind half the time."

"Just take my hand and trust me." Axen grabbed my hand and told me to shut my eyes. I did, and he pulled me along as he ran through the woods. It felt much farther than our usual jumps when he told me to open my eyes.

"Can you see?" he asked.

"Yes."

"Good, because I can't. If you keep your eyes shut in the shadows, it must not cause the vision change." Axen held out his hand again. "Your turn to lead."

I grabbed his hand and bolted through the next few streams of light. Alternating, we made it through the woods as the sun disappeared behind the horizon, leaving us with only the stars and a distant campfire to lead us to the camp. A woman came to greet us as we neared, and after some introductions, she invited us to join the group by the fire.

The woman disappeared inside a tent and soon returned with a book. "Here is your final clue," she said. "It is from my ancestor's copy of *The Adventures of Huckleberry Finn* by Mark Twain." She passed the book to me, and I opened to a marked page. Snuggling against Axen, I read aloud.

"'Stars and shadows ain't good to see by.'" I looked to Axen and smiled.

"What letters do we have now?" Axen asked.

I thought for a moment.

"We have an I, a W, a T, an F and an S. Mean anything to you?"

"Nope, but I'm sure Aldred will have some insight for us."

"Only a descendant of the author will have the Final Answer, and they themselves will have to say it," the woman told us. "I sure hope Aldred has the information you need. But for now, I think what you two need is some sleep."

***

Go to ENDING S on *page 219*

THROUGH THE WINTER FOREST—
GULLIVER'S TRAVELS

"I'd rather avoid the Answers training course," Axen said. "I'm sure that would bring back some bad memories."

"That's understandable." I turned to the old woman. "Any last-minute advice for us?"

"The answer will not be in the form of a written word, but rather from the heart of the author to the heart of Ashkelan." Her tone held an air of mystery.

"What do you mean the heart of Ashkelan?" I asked.

"The descendant will know," she said. I looked at Axen with confusion, but he didn't look very enlightened either. "Now take these and be on your way. You'll need to be warm in the winter forest." The woman handed us some scarves and hats.

Thanking our host, we headed out from the camp. Walking along the grassy terrain, Axen and I tried to keep the conversation lighthearted.

"What do you think you'll do once the Answers are defeated?" he asked.

"I don't know. Probably read every book I can get my hands on."

"Well, you said you would go back for your sister. Do you think she'll want to travel with you?"

"Oh, yes. Honestly, I'm a little worried about her," I said.

"Why's that?"

"My father. Ever since Mom died, he's turned into a monster. He never knew how to handle us girls, and when Mom got sick, he stopped trying. Next thing I knew, my sister and I had to be careful if he staggered as he walked in the door."

"I'm sorry," Axen said, turning to me. "How old were you?"

"When my mom passed? I was eleven. I took over the chores and house duties and rarely got out to spend time with friends or have a life of my own. To be honest, I hadn't been on a tower run in almost two years when I did it the day you found me."

"I can't imagine having to run a household at that age. I'm sure your sister appreciated you."

"We were close, though I doubt I told her as much. I'm worried about how she's managing without me. I was always the mediator between her and dad. I took the brunt of the damage so she wouldn't have to." I ran my thumb over a scar on my arm from the latest drunken rage. "So, what do you think the heart of Ashkelan is?"

Thankfully, Axen took the change of topic.

"I'm not sure. Possibly something at the Answers' headquarters. I know they have a control room. Or maybe the meeting room where the leaders make their decisions. Either of those are possibilities."

"What about the library?"

"That's true. I doubt we'll know much more about this answer until after we find the descendant."

"I would assume we've already run into the descendent at one of these camps."

We reached a small hill and started our way over.

"It's possible. Though I know there are some descendants

of authors living within the walls as well. Our only issue would be if the descendant has been inducted into the Answers. Then we would be back at square one."

"You don't think they'd remember the answer?"

"They wouldn't remember their last names to begin with, let alone something an ancestor said," Axen stated.

"How do you know it's something they would have said?"

"Well, the woman said the answer is from the heart of the author, and from the heart, the mouth speaks. So, I can only assume it's something they've said."

Hitting the top of the hill, I looked out and saw a beautiful forest splayed before me. White birch trees stood tall in the snow, their branches dripping with ice. The sun glittered off the white, and I could see small rainbows where the icicles refracted the light. The sight itself was enough to take my breath away even without the cold front that hit my lungs.

Pulling the scarf around my face and the hat over my ears, I headed toward the trail in the middle of the woods.

"It's beautiful here," I said, my voice muffled through the scarf.

"It is, but something tells me there has to be a catch." Axen's eyes remained wary as we entered the path.

My nose turned cold, and I wished I had some gloves. The snow soaked through my boots, making them feel even heavier as we trudged along.

"I'm not going to lie. I didn't expect it to be quite this cold." I could feel the bitter air down to my bones, and it felt as if they could break.

"I agree," Axen said. "I also didn't expect it to take this long to navigate through."

I looked over to respond and jumped back. "Axen! Your face!"

"What about it?"

"You have wrinkles!"

"What do you mean?" Axen lifted his hand to his cheeks, and his face flushed.

Wrinkled skin took the place of his former young face as if he had aged twenty years within minutes. Looking at me, Axen's jaw dropped. I reached up and felt what I feared. I had them too.

"What's happening?" I asked.

"The aging process must be faster in this realm. At this rate, we'll both die of old age before we reach the end of the forest. We need to hurry." Axen started to run but soon realized that his rapidly aging body wouldn't allow such quick movement.

"It's going to be difficult to rush when I can barely move without at least six things cracking." I tried to walk forward and felt clicks in my knees and a soreness in my joints.

"Now, I know what Aldred must feel like."

I chuckled at Axen's remark and pressed on. I could feel my hair turning brittle, and looking down, saw my soft, dark curls had turned a wiry white. My hands became weathered, and the cold started to feel more intimidating than ever.

After another hour of trekking through the drifts, I could feel my body starting to shut down, my now frail form giving in to the wicked atmosphere.

"Axen, I don't think I can go any farther." My voice sounded unfamiliar and distant as the air stole my words the moment they were said. Sinking to my knees, I could feel the snow melting beneath me. Succumbing to the cold, I curled up and shut my eyes. As I began to drift off, I felt Axen pick me up and force me to stand.

"You're not giving up on me now," he said. "Look, the exit is right there. You can make it."

I could vaguely see the sunlight marking the end of this treacherous forest. Stumbling along with the support of my elderly companion, I pushed through to the end of the woods. As we stepped onto the warm grass, I collapsed to the ground.

After several minutes, I felt my strength returning and looked at my hands to see they had returned to their youthfulness. I tried to stand and found my bones felt strong and nothing creaked within me as I moved. Axen had regained his handsome physique as well, and we both turned to look back at the woods.

"I guess it only ages you while you're in there?" I wondered aloud.

"Thankfully, yes. I wasn't ready to give up my good looks just yet." Axen stretched his muscles.

I snorted. "Sure. That would have been the greatest concern. I rolled my eyes and then focused on a camp in the near distance.

As we neared, a woman came to greet us, and we filled her in on our story. Inviting us back to her tent, she rattled on about the answer.

"This should be your last clue," she said. "Then, you'll need to get back to Aldred. He'll be able to decipher it. I can't believe we might finally be free of the Answers. I never would've dreamed I'd see the day."

We sat at her table, and she offered us something to eat while she pulled a book from a nearby shelf. She pushed it across the table for us to see, and I looked down at the cover. *Gulliver's Travels* by Jonathan Swift. Opening to a marked page, I read aloud.

"'Every man desires to live long, but no man wishes to be old.'" I snorted. "After today, I can agree with that."

"So that leaves us with a W, an S, an I, an L, and now an E." Axen rattled off our clues as the woman served us something to eat.

"You can head to Aldred in the morning. He knows all the authors of old. But for now, eat up."

***

Turn to ENDING L *on page 225*

THROUGH THE TRAINING COURSE—
THE PRINCESS BRIDE

"I think the training course would be interesting to see," Axen said. "I know what the updated ones look like, but I'd like to see an original."

"Just remember they are dangerous. They were built to drive out the weak when it came to minds. Stay strong, and you should make it through," the old woman said.

"We'll be careful," I said.

"Do you have any other information for us about the Final Answer?" Axen asked.

"Well, dears, once you get all five clues, get back to Aldred. He will know how to decipher it, and then you'll need to find the descendant. Only they will know the answer. Then, you must make your way back to Ashkelan. I can only hope that the descendant is easy to find."

"Well, I guess we should be on our way then." Axen stood and thanked our host before turning to leave. Giving the old woman a quick hug, I followed, and we headed toward a small hill in the distance.

"So, what are the training courses like now at headquarters?" I asked.

"Well, the simple ones are built like an obstacle course. They are only there to test your strength and abilities after undergoing the electromagnetic therapy. The more advanced courses mess with your mind. They keep you hooked to the therapy machines, and if you make the wrong choice, you get shocked."

"Is that what those scars are from?" I pointed to starburst-shaped burn marks on Axen's forearms.

"Yes." He pulled his sleeves down to cover them. "Since I kept my ability to read, the courses were more difficult. I had to go against everything I would have thought."

"That must have been difficult."

"It was. Like the woman at the camp said, they were made to weed out the weak. Though it would be easier to say it was meant to destroy the strong. If you could beat the therapy, the course would tear you up."

"So, it was meant to see how brainwashed the minions were."

"Exactly."

Axen and I continued up the hill in silence as my mind tried to wrap around all the cruelty the Answers dealt.

How could a simple group of scientists become that afraid? Surely the readers were peaceful. I can't imagine any of the readers I've met so far meaning any harm. Hearing my own thoughts inside my head had become a great comfort, and I wondered how I'd lived my whole life without them.

Thinking back to my time growing up in Ashkelan, I had always known something was different about me. My mother said I got her adventurous spirit. Dad would call me a rebel which was much nicer than the terms he used when not sober.

I need to get back to my sister. I don't know how she's surviving Dad with me gone.

"Axen, do you know how we'll get back into the city?"

"No clue. I'm hoping Aldred will know. Why?" Axen turned to look at me.

"I need to get my sister out. She shouldn't be left alone with my dad. I never should have left without her."

"Calessa, you left because you had to. Now, you are trying to make the world a better place for her. I'm sure she'll understand. Why can't she be left alone with your dad?"

I looked down. "Let's just say Dad doesn't know how to act around us. He spends more time at the tavern than with us, and when he's home, he's rarely sober. I mediate between them. Without me there, there's no one to protect her."

"Well, I'm sure as soon as we find the descendant we will be headed back, and you'll be able to go to her."

When we reached the top of the hill, I looked down to see the training course not too far in the distance. Obstacles stood at every angle, and some seemed unavoidable to get through. I turned to Axen. His eyes blazed as he walked. I assumed the course was not bringing back good memories.

"You going to be okay?" I asked.

"Yeah." He blinked and twitched his head. "Just some aftershocks. I'll be fine. I'm more worried about you, to be honest."

"I'm sure I'll be fine."

At the entrance of the course stood a sign with a roughly drawn map of the obstacles and a warning.

"'Readers beware, or you'll fall into the snare,'" I read.

A shiver ran down my spine as we stepped up to the first obstacle. A tall wall stood in front of us with ropes hanging from the top and a small sign posted in the center.

"It says 'up and over,'" I said.

"I think we should go around." Axen pointed.

I turned and saw that the wall stretched for at least a mile in both directions.

"Don't be silly. It'll be faster to climb." I started up the rope. Climbing up the wall proved easy, and soon, I was almost to the top, but looking at the upper edge, my face drained. I now knew why Axen had suggested the long way. As I climbed, my weight had pulled my rope down onto a sharp razor, cutting it with every move. Gasping, I tried to grab the top of the wall, but I was too late. My rope snapped, and I plummeted back to the ground. Landing on top of Axen with a thud, we slammed onto the ground. I rolled off and coughed as I stood.

"I'm so sorry, are you okay?" I asked.

"I'm fine." Axen stood and dusted off his pants. "Next time, listen to the ex-Answer. I knew it had to be a trap. This course is meant to mess with readers, remember. Do as you're told, not what you read."

I nodded, and we began our long walk around the wall.

Almost an hour later, we reached the end. Turning the corner, we saw our next obstacle: a wooden tunnel. Inside, I could see small metal spikes peeking from the walls. The entrance looked as if it could trigger the mechanisms within the walls, and a sign outside with the word DANGER proved my concern.

"Come on," Axen said, grabbing my hand and pulling.

I stood frozen.

"Why wouldn't we just go around?" I asked. The grass on either side looked safe.

"This is why." Axen picked up a rock and tossed it to the side of the tunnel. As it landed, the ground crumbled beneath it to reveal a deep pit. I gasped and stepped back as the ground fell. "Now, let's go."

Axen tugged on my arm again, and we entered the corridor. I shut my eyes and prepared for the worst, but no sharp pricks attacked my skin. I opened my eyes and saw that Axen was already near the end. I rushed to catch up to him.

The rest of the course was similar. Messages of shortcuts or dangers tried to deceive me as I followed Axen's every word. When we'd made it through, I let out a breath I hadn't known I was holding.

"Thank you," I said. "I would've died going through that on my own."

"Well, I guess it's lucky I've been brainwashed before." Axen smirked and pointed up ahead. The camp wasn't far off, and we headed toward it as the sun sank beneath the ground.

A large campfire lit our way, and soon, we were greeted by a group of men and women.

"Who are you?" one woman asked.

We made our introductions and told our story. Soon, we were invited to sit around the fire. The woman offered us something to eat as Axen and I huddled close to the warmth.

"You two look like you've had a long day," she said. "But don't worry, it was a worthy trip. I do believe I have your final clue." She disappeared into her tent and came back a moment later with a book. She handed the book to me, and I read the cover aloud.

"*The Princess Bride* by S. Morgenstern." I flipped the book open to a marked page and read the underlined quote. "'Existence was really very simple when you did what you were told.'" Thinking for a moment, I thought back on all our clues. "A W, an S, an I, an L, and an E. Why do those letters seem familiar?"

"I don't recognize them," Axen said. "But I'm sure Aldred will know."

"Oh, I'm sure he will," the woman said. "But please, don't try to leave tonight. You can stay here and get a fresh start in the daylight."

***

Turn to ENDING L *on page 225*

THROUGH THE ENCHANTED
VILLAGE—THE SECRET GARDEN

"Let's go through the enchanted village," Axen said, looking at the map.

"I was hoping you'd say that." I smiled at the thought of what it might look like.

"The enchanted village holds many secrets," the old woman said. "Only a powerful reader will be able to unlock the mysteries."

"What mysteries?" I asked, my eyes wide.

"Oh, I don't know. I've never been there," the woman stated.

I chuckled. "Well, I guess I'll have to wait and see."

"Do you have anything else you can tell us about the Final Answer before we leave?" Axen asked.

"The answer won't be found in a book or on parchment, but from within the author."

"If the author knew the answer, why didn't they use it while they were still alive?" I asked.

"I can only imagine it has to do with how powerful the Answers are. Maybe they thought the world would resort right back to its wicked ways."

"Then why do it now?"

"Because I believe the world is better than it was. And you two are living proof. You chose freedom, and you chose to help the others without worry for your own lives. That kind of selflessness and hope tells me the world is ready to be set free." The old woman patted my hand.

"I think we should be on our way." Axen stood as he spoke. "Thank you for everything." Nodding at the old woman, he turned and headed out from the camp. I said my goodbye and followed as we walked toward a small hill.

"Do you think the world will be able to survive without the Answers? I mean, most of us have never lived without them," I said.

"I don't see why not. I think once people remember what they've been missing all these years, the world will thrive. Can you imagine if Ashkelan had bookstores and public libraries? People could even write letters to each other again." Axen's blue eyes turned bright.

"If people could write, then maybe there could be new books!" His excitement felt contagious. "Wait, can I write?"

"Anyone can. If you can read, you can write."

"Can you imagine writing about this? Making a story of all our adventures?"

Axen chuckled, and I was glad to have such a positive start to the afternoon. The heat beat into my skin, but I didn't mind. We were close to the Final Answer, I could feel it.

Maybe by this time tomorrow, you'll be back in Ashkelan, setting everyone free. That is, if we can find the descendant.

"Do you think you'll stay in Ashkelan after this is all over?" Axen's words broke through my voice's lament, and I looked over at him.

"Maybe. I know I want to go back for my sister, but I think I may bring her out here into the world. I'm sure she would love to see it. How about you?"

"I guess it will depend on if I can ever remember my family. Though I doubt I'd be happy living within those stone walls again."

"I couldn't agree more. My mother always told me there was more out there than what I could see. I always thought she meant figuratively, but maybe she knew all along." My eyes got misty talking about my mom. I missed her.

"It's always possible. I wouldn't be surprised if there were some readers hiding under the Answers' noses."

"So, what do you think the enchanted village will be like?" I asked, done with the more serious topic.

"I don't know, but we're about to find out," Axen said as we reached the top of the hill.

My mind spun at the sight before me. The small village below glistened in the sun causing the buildings to look as if they were made of light. Iridescent and glittering, the town stood proud in the middle of its realm. The grass even had a shimmer to it as the magic seeped from the sides of the buildings. The streets were paved with prisms, and I could see tiny rainbows dancing their way through the town square.

"It's incredible," I breathed.

"I don't know if that's the word I would use for it." Axen's tone caused me to turn, and I saw his eyes had turned to a scowl.

"What do you mean?" I asked. "It's beautiful!"

"Beautiful?" Axen grunted. "You think a rundown village in the middle of nowhere is beautiful?"

"Rundown? Axen, what does this place look like to you?"

"The buildings are dark and falling apart. The roads are cracked and dirty, and the grass is dead. Why? What do you see?"

"Not that." My eyes grew wide as I looked back at the majestic view. "It's a paradise. Bright and wonderful. I can't even begin to explain it."

"Well, I guess maybe that's how it's enchanted."

"But why can I see it and you can't?"

"Hold on, there's a sign here." Axen walked over to the side of the road, but I saw no sign. "It says 'The one who believes, sees'" Axen paused. "Believes in what?"

"Magic maybe?" I asked.

"But I know there is magic. I've seen enough of it on this trip." I saw Axen's frustration grow.

"Maybe you know it in your head, but your heart doesn't grasp the possibilities." I tried to speak softly, careful of what words I chose. "You know, there's a difference in knowing something and putting your faith in it."

"I guess you might be right. I have to admit, I was hesitant to believe this place was going to be enchanted to begin with. Maybe if you don't believe it from the start, you can't see its true form."

"Well, I'm sorry you're missing out. But I promise to tell you all about it as we go."

As we headed farther into the village, I paused occasionally to tell Axen what I saw. When we reached the center of the town square, I approached a huge fountain in the middle. The glass monument spewed light rather than water, the luminescent drops splashing into a pool of sunshine. I began to read the small plaque on the side.

"'If one wants a second chance, toss a coin without a glance.' Hey, Axen, throw a coin in this fountain over here."

"What fountain? All I see is a pile of rubble."

"Just trust me."

Axen begrudgingly pulled a coin from his pocket and tossed it into the fountain. The splash was so bright, I had to shield my eyes. When I opened them, I noticed that Axen's eyes had grown wide. He looked around in wonder, and I knew it had worked.

"Isn't it incredible?" I asked.

"Yes." He looked at me. "Thank you."

"Of course. What are friends for?" I smiled, and we started through the rest of the village.

Soon, we were looking out at the camp in the distance. Their campfire helped guide us as dusk set in, and we reached the group of men and women huddled by the flames. Introducing ourselves quickly, we were invited to join the campers, and we relayed our journey up to this point.

"I think I have your final clue," a woman said. She hurried to a tent and returned with a book. "This is *The Secret Garden* by Frances Hodgson Burnett. I think you'll find your quote here."

Handing the book to Axen, he opened it and read the quote aloud.

"'Everything is made out of magic, leaves and trees, flowers and birds, badgers and foxes and squirrels and people. So, it must be all around us.'"

"So now, we have a W, an S, an I, an L, and an E," I said.

"I wish I could tell you the author's name," the woman said. "But sadly, I'm not familiar with all the authors of old."

"That's okay," I said. "We'll head to Aldred first thing in the morning."

***

Turn to ENDING L *on page 225*

AROUND THE VOLCANO—THE
PILGRIM'S PROGRESS

"Going around the volcano will be a faster route." Axen's nose was buried in the map.

"Are you sure it's safe, though?" I asked.

"It should be," the old woman said. "It's been dormant for well over one hundred years."

"See? We'll be fine," Axen stated.

"All right, well, is there anything else we should know before we leave?" I turned to the old woman.

"Just remember to always follow your heart, my dear. It is rarely wrong." The old woman grabbed my hand. "I see something special in you. I know the world is in good hands with you two."

Axen and I thanked our host and headed out of the camp in the afternoon sun.

"Do you think we'll make it to the next camp by dark?" I asked.

"I don't see why not. It shouldn't take too long to get around the volcano." Axen led the way up a nearby hill.

"I'm not sure what she expects of me, but I don't think I can live up to whatever it was." I thought back on what the old woman had said.

"Well, you are a reader. So that makes you special to begin with."

"Yes, I know. But then why did she say it to me and not you?"

"I don't know." Axen shrugged.

I let my mind wander, and soon, it replayed childhood memories as moving pictures in my mind—playing with my sister, listening to my mother sing, and helping her cook dinner each night. The reminiscent smile faded though as the timeline progressed—Mom getting sick, her passing, and then Dad drinking, yelling, fighting. My face grew solemn as my brain chose to play out memories I'd have rather forgotten. A small gasp escaped my lips as my hand went to the scar from the latest battle.

"Calessa, are you okay?" Axen asked.

"What?" I snapped out of my unsettling memories and looked at Axen. "Oh, yes. I'm fine."

"You don't seem fine."

"Well, I am. Just thinking about home. I'm anxious to get back to my sister. That's all. My mind tried to play unknown scenarios of what may be going on with me gone, but I forced them to stop."

"You seem very devoted to her." Axen smiled.

"I am. Ever since Mom passed, I've taken care of her."

"What about your father?"

"He did little more than bring home the money. But I'd rather not talk about it."

"All right, I'm sorry."

"It's okay. So, do you know how we'll get back into Ashkelan? I'm guessing that tunnel will be guarded now."

"I have no clue. I'm sure Aldred will have something to help though. Or it's always possible that the descendant may know something we don't."

"Where do you think we'll find them?"

"Could be anywhere. For all I know, we may have to travel all the realms again searching for them. Or they could be inside the walls already."

"This could take years." My spirits sank at the thought.

"I don't know. I have a good feeling about it. And honestly, we need to hurry. The Answers are getting more aggressive in their inductions."

I sighed as we crested the hill. The volcano rose before me. I looked up at the blackened rock, and a waft of smoky air hit my nose.

"Look, there's a path that leads through the center of the volcano." Axen pointed to a cavern opening in the center of the mountain.

As we neared, I could barely see into the dark corridor.

"I think we should go around like we planned. That doesn't look too safe."

"Who are you kidding? That passageway could cut over an hour off our journey. We should go through."

"But what if the volcano erupts?"

"The woman said it's been dormant for years. We'll be fine."

I eyed the stalactites hanging from the ceiling. The walls appeared to be made of magma from a previous eruption. I could envision the lava running behind the walls, and I shivered at the thought of it bursting through.

"You're crazy to go in there."

"I'm going this way. You're welcome to go around if you're that worried." Axen started into the tunnel, and I let my frustration rise.

"Well, fine," I stated. "I'll see you on the other side then." Turning away, I started to walk around the base of the volcano, mumbling to myself as I went. *Why should I care if he wants to risk his life? At least I know I'm safe. One of us has to be smart about this.* My mind switched from griping to worry. *I hope he's safe in there. I hope the volcano doesn't erupt. Though I'm sure it will be—*

Looking up, I gasped. A thin spiral of smoke curled from the opening of the mountain. *It's active!* My mind raced as I watched the smoke grow thicker. A low rumble hit my ears, and I started to run. Rushing toward the far end of the mountain, I screamed.

"Axen! Axen, can you hear me?" I received no response. Sprinting, I tried to keep up my strength, but it was much farther around the volcano than I anticipated. I started to understand Axen's wish for a shorter journey. My head pounded in rhythm with my heart as my body grew tired and worn. Looking up every so often, I saw the smoke billowing from the top as the rumbling grew.

I turned a corner and prayed to see Axen there waiting for me, but he was nowhere to be seen. I yelled again.

"Axen!"

"Calessa!" I heard his call from within the tunnel, and I rushed forward. Not too far in, Axen lay on the ground, his leg bleeding from where a stalactite had fallen and pierced his thigh.

I knelt and pulled the spike from his leg, tying my jacket around his leg to stop the bleeding.

"There was an earthquake. I lost my balance, and the stalactite fell before I could move."

"It wasn't an earthquake." I helped Axen to his feet and helped him hobble toward the exit. "The volcano is erupting."

"What?" Axen's face flushed.

"Yes, I could see the smoke from outside. We need to hurry."

Pulling Axen along, I reached the opening as the whole ground began to shake. I looked up and saw the volcano burst. Molten lava flew sky high, as bright as the sun. Axen and I scrambled away and up a hill to avoid the flow as the lava plunged down the mountain, eating everything in its path.

Looking ahead, we could see the camp in the distance and made our way there. A woman came to meet us.

"What happened? Are you two all right?" she asked.

"No, he's hurt." I motioned to Axen's leg.

"Come this way."

"What about the volcano? It will destroy the camp." My voice cracked As anxious breaths filled my lungs.

"The camp is safe. Look." The woman pointed back to the erupting mountain. The lava had slowed, and the magma that still cascaded down poured liked a waterfall into a wide trench in the ground. "We had that dug when we first set up camp. It was safe to travel over, but the heat of the lava burned through the makeshift top allowing the ground to channel the danger away."

My breathing slowed at the sight and the woman welcomed us into her tent. After doctoring Axen's leg, she offered us something to eat.

"Now, would you two like to tell me who you are and what brought you here?"

I filled the woman in on our journey, and she scurried over to a shelf. Pulling out a book, she returned and handed the manuscript to me. I traced my finger over the elaborate cover. *The Pilgrim's Progress* by John Bunyan. Opening to a marked page, I read the quote aloud.

"'Everyone needs to make his own choices.'" I looked at Axen and he looked down at the floor.

"Maybe I shouldn't have made my own choice today, at least," he said.

"Well, no use worrying about it now. Where does that leave us on clues?"

"W, S, I, L, and E," Axen said.

"Any ideas on what it spells?" I asked.

"No, but Aldred will know."

"Rest tonight," the woman said. "You can leave in the morning."

***

ONCE UPON A BOOK

Turn to ENDING L *on page 225*

ENDING T

The next morning, Axen and I got an early start to make our way back toward the base camp. Axen mumbled to himself as we walked, though I couldn't quite make out what he was saying.

"What's on your mind?" I asked.

"Those letters. Something is familiar about them, but I don't know why. It's like my mind is trying to remember something important."

"Do you think you know who the author is?"

"Maybe. But if I do, I've forgotten."

"How long will it take to reach the base camp?" I asked.

Axen consulted the map. "Apparently not very long. It looks as if we've traveled in a circle. The shoreline is just over this next hill."

The smell of saltwater wafted in on the morning breeze as we neared the beach. It had been quite a while since I had first seen the ocean, but the amazement hit me just as it did before. Reaching the sand, I realized how much had changed since we had been here last. I breathed deep as we headed to the camp entrance. As we reached the gate, Aldred came hobbling to meet us.

"Did you find it?" Aldred's eyes lit up.

"Sort of," I said. "We have clues as to who the author is that has the Final Answer. But we don't know how to decipher it."

"Well, come in, come in. I'm sure I can help with that." Aldred rushed us inside and over to his home. "You have no idea how happy I am to see you two. I was starting to fear the worst." The old man fixed us some tea and sat down across from us. "Now, how can I help?"

Axen pulled a sheet of parchment out of his pocket that had the letters scrawled on it. "We have these five letters, and they are supposed to spell an author's name. But we don't know which one."

Aldred picked up the paper. "W, T, I, A, N. Why, this is referring to Mark Twain!" He stood and walked to his bookshelf. He returned a few moments later with a large book. "This is a collection of Mark Twain's greatest stories. *Tom Sawyer, The Adventures of Huckleberry Finn,* and more. I wonder if the Final Answer has been under my nose this whole time. If only I knew of one of his descendants. Hmph."

Aldred began scouring the pages, and I looked over to Axen.

"You said the letters sounded familiar. Ring any bells?" I asked.

"I'm not sure." His hands swiped down his face.

"Mark Twain was only a pen name," Aldred explained. "His real name was Samuel Clemens."

Axen's eyes blitzed. "My last name is Clemens. I'm the descendant."

Aldred clapped his hands together. "Well then, you must know where to find the Final Answer. Where is it? Is it in one of his works?"

Axen furrowed his brow and shut his eyes. "I don't remember. I didn't know about any of his books. Wait. I remember something. An old family saying that was passed down from generation to generation." He eyes opened and an excitement filled them. "'The two most important days in your life are the day you are born and the day you find out why.'"

"That's it!" Aldred jumped from his seat. "That has to be. I can feel it in my bones!" He did a little jig around the table before returning to his seat. "Now, the only question left is how to get you back inside the walls." He scurried over to another shelf and brought back a small piece of parchment. As he laid it on the table, I saw a detailed drawing of Ashkelan and its walls. It showed the tunnel we had traveled through as well as a duct work built into the siding.

"Where does that tunnel lead?"

"That's headquarters," Axen said. "It looks like an air duct they use to keep the headquarters ventilated. That may be our only way in. However, it looks like it comes down right in the drone's area. Everyone there will either be brainless or taking care of the brainless."

"Well then, maybe it will be easy to sneak in?" I suggested.

"Ah, but you have to make your way to the heart of Ashkelan," Aldred chimed in.

"Where's that?" I asked.

"My guess would be the control panel. There's a room near the drones that holds the main computer and all the surveillance. I bet I could use the system to shout the answer over the speakers." Axen stood. "We better get going. No reason to wait around."

Aldred sent us off with the map to the duct and promises to tell us more about Axen's ancestor after this whole mess was cleaned up. Reaching the vent, Axen and I heaved the metal grate to the side and climbed in. Following the route, I felt the anxiety of being so close to the enemy. Commanding voices mixed with mechanisms beeping and whirring almost covered the screams that reached my ears.

"Where's the screaming coming from?" I whispered.

"People going through the electromagnetic therapy for the first time. It isn't a pleasant experience."

Soon, we were hovering above the grate that led into the headquarters. Looking down, I could see people of all ages milling around—their bodies almost swallowed by the white jumpsuits they wore. No one spoke, but only murmured and moaned as they roamed about, knocking into each other as they went. The sight sent shivers down my spine.

"How do you expect to get through?"

"I have a plan. But I'm going to need you to follow my lead." Axen silently moved the grate. I watched as he slipped through and onto the top bunk of a bed nearby. Following, I realized that not a single drone had turned to see. Their eyes looked bloodshot and sunken. Odd-shaped scars mapped their temples and hands.

Once on the ground, Axen grabbed two extra jumpsuits from a rack and handed one to me, motioning to put it on over my clothes. I did, and we began to sneak through the main floor to the door on the other side. Voices interrupted our plans and Axen pulled me to the side.

"Act like them," he whispered before the door swung open, and two women in white suits entered.

I looked at Axen and saw that he stared straight ahead and started to roam around. I followed his lead, keeping an eye on the two women.

"Drone duty is the worst," one woman said.

"I know. All they do is moan and groan as if their life has been ruined. As if there is anything to live for anyway," the other said. She poked a drone, causing it to lose balance and topple to the floor.

"Hey, this one looks new." The first woman stared at Axen as he milled about. I felt a surge of fear but managed to keep my emotions inside my head.

"He must have been sent down last shift." The second woman paid little attention to him. "Come on, let's go. It's time for lunch anyway." The two women left, and Axen pushed his way through the drones to me.

"That was close," I said.

"Yeah, thankfully, I happen to know that the whole floor takes lunch at the same time. Come on." Axen made his way to the door.

Peeking through the window, he nodded his head and opened the door quietly. We snuck down the connected hallway for a few feet before Axen ducked into a room, pulling me with him.

Large frames showing moving pictures lined the walls, showing every inch of the headquarters—torture rooms, meeting areas, and more stretched across every wall in full display. I had never seen technology this advanced. I gaped at the items a bit before noticing Axen flipping switches and turning knobs. Grabbing a stick with a soft knob at the end, he spoke.

"Attention Answers! This is Axen Clemens speaking, descendant of Mark Twain, and you need to hear what I have to say." Axen took a deep breath and quoted his ancestor in a clear tone. "'The two most important days in your life are the day you are born and the day you find out why.'"

Static filled the screens for a moment and then cleared, showing different scenes. Gone were the images of torture and people milling about in a mindless daze. Now we saw Answers and minions talking to each other as if they had just met—smiles spread across their faces. They were finally free.

"Now what?" I asked.

"Now, we start off this new world on the right foot. And I think we should begin by getting out of these walls once and for all."

Axen's eyes flashed a brighter blue before settling into the color of the sky. He was finally free too.

THE END

ENDING S

The following morning, Axen and I got an early start back toward Aldred.

"It should only take us a few hours to make it back to base camp." Axen walked with his nose in the map.

"Really? How did they not know there was a camp so close by?" I asked.

"I guess when the map got split up, they never bothered to explore much outside of what they were familiar with. I can't say I blame them."

The voice chattered as we navigated back to the beach. *I can't believe how different I am from when I was last here. Before, we were a fugitive and a confused girl. Now look at us.* Axen and I walked hand in hand toward the sound of ocean waves.

"Axen, did you ever expect to be here?" I asked.

"Here as in outside Ashkelan? Or here as in with you?" He nudged me playfully.

"Both."

"Honestly, no. After I was conscripted, I thought my life was over. It took everything in me not to give in and let myself become a minion like the rest of them."

"Well, I'm glad you didn't." I reached up to kiss him on the cheek and he blushed at my touch.

As we walked over a small hill, my boots hit the familiar sand. Breathing in the fresh salty air brought me back to the excitement of when I first saw the beautiful ocean.

We made our way to Aldred's home and were met at the door with his big smile.

"Welcome back," Aldred said. "I see you two have gotten to know each other." He winked at Axen and I smiled.

"We think we have the next part to the Final Answer," Axen said. "One author holds the key, and we found clues of who the author might be. We were hoping you could help."

"Give me the clues, and I'll see what I can do."

"We have a group of letters. We have an I, a W, a T, an F and an S," I stated. Aldred's face went white as he stared at us, his mouth hanging open. "Aldred, are you all right?"

The old man shut his mouth and hobbled over to his bookshelf. He pulled an ancient book from the top shelf and carried it back to the table, muttering to himself the whole time.

"Do you know who the author is?" Axen asked.

Ignoring us, Aldred flipped through his book for a while before looking up.

"I've had the answer under my nose the whole time," he said.

"What do you mean?" I asked.

"The author is Swift. Jonathan Swift. And I am Aldred Swift. I'm the descendant." He showed us the cover. "This is Jonathan Swift's book *Gulliver's Travels*. The answer must be in here somewhere." He went back to flipping through the pages and mumbling before gasping and turning to the front page.

"Here!" he said. "Something Jonathan always used to say. This is the Final Answer, I can feel it. He even wrote it in the inscription of this book. 'Vision is the art of seeing things invisible.'"

"Great! Now we have to figure out how to get us all into Ashkelan." Axen stood and paced the floor.

"I might have a solution for that." Aldred pulled a map from a box and laid it out on the table. A blueprint of Ashkelan was drawn in detail before me.

"Do you think we could make it through the drainpipes or something?" I asked.

"Oh no, I'm much too old for that!" Aldred chuckled. "I was thinking more of entering through the trash dock here toward the back of Answers Headquarters."

"That could work!" Axen rushed back to the table. "I used to work on the trash docks. There's a large bay door that opens to the compound. I never thought about the fact that there must have been a door to the outside there."

"So, you mean to tell me we could have avoided having to deal with the wall altogether when we escaped?" I glared at Axen.

"Uh, yeah. Sorry." Axen pushed a hand through his hair.

"Well," Aldred clapped his hands. "Let's go!"

We followed the spunky old man out of the camp.

"Aldred, we know the quote has to be spoken at the heart of Ashkelan. Do you know where that might be?" I asked.

"Ah, yes. The library. We need to get to the library. Can you help with that?" He looked at Axen.

"Yeah, I can get us there. We'll just have to be careful not to be caught."

Reaching the compound, I looked up at the large metal structure off the side of the wall. Axen found a small door and pried it open to reveal a smell I doubted I'd forget. A stench wafted from the area and permeated the air around us. Plugging our noses, we entered the sea of trash and started to make our way toward the bay door, careful not to make a sound.

"Now what?" I asked. "The door's closed."

"Just wait. They open it every fifteen minutes to throw more trash out. When they do, follow my lead."

Sure enough, a few minutes later, the wide bay door lifted to reveal two men in dirty white jumpsuits tossing garbage into the giant pile. Axen motioned us to the side, and we climbed up over the edge, helping Aldred up as we went.

Staying to the side of the room, we snuck around to the opposing door and bolted through it and into an empty hall. I looked to Axen for our next move. He motioned us to stay low and quiet as he led us down the sterile hallways. Stopping in between two metal doors, Axen pressed on the wall, and a panel slid to reveal a passageway. Climbing in, we all sighed in relief as he closed the panel behind us.

"Is this the same tunnel we were in?" I whispered.

"Yes, but I knew they wouldn't guard it this far back. We still need to make it to the library without being caught, though."

Creeping down the tunnel, I could hear the Answers' operation from beyond the walls. Machines whirred and people screamed. Voices carried as they talked, though I couldn't make out their words. When we'd reached the right panel, Axen pulled a handle, and the wall slid open to reveal the space where this had all begun.

I stepped into the library and my eyes grew as big as they did the first time. I could feel my heartbeat in my throat as I let my fingers run across the spines of the books. If only I could stay here and read them all. I looked over and saw Aldred mesmerized by the books. He looked at Axen and me and choked up.

"I never thought I would get the chance to see this many books in one place again. Let alone the day we're all set free."

A loud crash disrupted the moment from outside the library and Axen looked at us with wide eyes.

"You might still not live to see it if we don't hurry. Guards are on their way."

Aldred headed to the center of the room. Guards burst through the doors and Aldred shouted, "'Vision is the art of seeing things invisible!'"

FAITH WEAVER

The guards froze in their steps and stumbled back. They blinked and looked at each other a few moments and then looked to us with a haze in their eyes.

"What happened?" one asked.

"I believe, good sir, that you just remembered what you'd forgotten," Aldred said.

The guards still looked dumbfounded but soon realized they were free to leave and ran out. I looked to Axen, and his bright eyes were filled with love as he returned the glance.

"Thank you, Aldred. I think the world is going to be a much better place from here on." Axen walked over, picked me up, and spun me around. Setting me down with a kiss, he smiled. "And as for you, milady. I thinks it's about time I took you home to meet my parents."

I smiled. This had turned into the greatest story I could have ever told.

THE END

ENDING L

Axen and I shuffled through the dew-covered grass. Morning had come much too quickly, and we had hurried to eat breakfast before making our way back toward the beach.

"You look like you have something on your mind. Everything okay?" Axen glanced at me he spoke.

"Yeah, I'm all right. Just thinking about the clues. Something is familiar about the letters, but I can't figure out what."

"Well, considering you've only started reading, you probably can't unscramble the letters in your mind yet. I'm sure it will come with time."

"I hope so." I inched closer to Axen. "Can I see the map? I want to see how far we have to the base camp."

He handed over the map. The camps we had visited were spotted around the parchment, and it appeared we were only a few hours from the camp.

"We went in a big circle."

"What?" Axen looked over my shoulder. "Huh. I guess we did."

"With the map split, they never would have known they were so close."

We reached the beach, and my boots felt much steadier on the sand than when I'd first stepped foot on the grainy land. Thinking back to all the terrain we had covered and how much I had changed, I wondered at the difference one week could make. *I'm not the same person I was when this all began.*

As we reached the entrance to the camp, Aldred came to meet us at the gate. He hobbled his way over the small bridge, his smile beaming.

"Did you find it? Are we free?" he asked.

"Not quite," I said apologetically. "But we're close. We need you to help us decipher some clues."

"Oh, wonderful! Come along then."

Hurrying us back to his house, Aldred asked all sorts of questions about our trip and then listened intently as we filled him in. Once inside, we gathered around his table, and Axen gave Aldred the clues.

"We have a W, an S, an I, an L, and an E. Can you decipher it?"

"Hmm, now let me think." Aldred walked to a shelf and ran his finger across the spines of the countless books. Exclaiming, he pulled a book from the shelf and returned to the table.

"*The Chronicles of Narnia* by C. S. Lewis. Why didn't I think of it before?" I could feel the blood drain from my face as I stared at Aldred.

"Calessa, are you okay?" Axen asked.

"Did you say Lewis?" I asked.

"Yes, why? Do you know the descendant?" Aldred looked at me with eager eyes.

"I'm the descendant. My mother's maiden name was Lewis." My mind tried to wrap around what was happening, and my breath caught in my throat.

"So then, you must know the answer!" Axen said as Aldred clapped his hands with excitement.

"I ... I guess I should. But I can't think of it." I thought hard. "Wait. There was something my mother would always say. She said it was a family saying."

"What was it?" Both Aldred and Axen said at the same time. I teared up as the voices repeated the quote in my mother's voice.

"'There are far, far better things ahead than any we leave behind,'" I said, blinking back tears. Sniffing, I looked at Aldred. "Do you know how we can get inside Ashkelan? I need to get to the heart of the city. I need to get to the town square."

"Why the town square?" Axen asked.

"I just have a feeling. So, Aldred, do you know?"

"Yes, I do. Look here." Aldred pulled a piece of paper from his shelf and laid it out on the table. A drawing of Ashkelan lay before us. I searched the map for an entrance but only spotted what would be the now-guarded tunnel.

"What am I missing?" I asked.

"The drainpipe," Axen stated. He pointed to the edge of the wall that lay in the middle of the ocean.

"And how are we supposed to get there?" I asked.

"I have a raft. You can use that to get to the pipe and then climb straight up into the city," Aldred said.

"Okay, then I guess we better get moving," Axen said, heading outside.

I followed, and Aldred showed us where his raft was stored. Thankfully, it wasn't too heavy, and Axen and I carried it out onto the beach. Careful not to make too much ruckus, we avoided the guards' patrolling eyes as we slipped it into the water and climbed aboard. Staying close to the wall, we floated in the shadows around the sides to the wall that held the drain.

"How are we going to get up into the pipe?" I asked, spotting the large tube several feet above my head.

"I'll help you up and then climb in after."

Axen gave me a boost, and I pulled myself into the tunnel. There hadn't been much rain, so the pipe was only damp, though a musty smell made it unpleasant. Axen hoisted himself up, and we started our way through the tunnel.

Reaching the grate beneath the city, I looked up to see the busy town bustling with life.

"How are we going to do this?" Axen whispered.

"I guess I'll climb up and get to the center of the town square and shout. I don't know. You got any better ideas?"

"None. Let's go."

A steel ladder along the side of the pipe made for an easy climb to the street. Pushing the grate aside, Axen and I climbed up onto the cobblestone. A few people gave us odd looks, but none bothered to stop. I was about to make my way toward the center of the city when I heard a voice from behind.

"Calessa!" I turned to see my sister running toward me.

Wrapping her in my arms, I hugged her as hard as I could.

"I'm so sorry I left, but I'm here now. Everything is going to be okay," I whispered to her as she sobbed into my shirt. She pulled back and looked at me with her big eyes, and then jumped when we heard another familiar voice.

"Calessa!" This one was laced with anger. "Where have you been? You think you can leave without a word? What were you thinking?"

My father stomped toward us. Instincts propelled me to push my sister behind me. Axen stepped up, his muscles tensed, but I pushed him back too.

"I've got this." My voice stayed level. "I'm sorry, Dad, but you aren't going to hurt us any longer. I'm sorry I left without saying anything, but I didn't have a choice. Now, if you'll excuse me, I have something to do."

I turned to walk away, but his rough grip captured my wrist, forcing me to turn around. I looked into his drunken eyes for only a moment before I ripped my arm from his grasp. Pulling my sister behind me, I ignored my father's outraged screams as I turned toward the town square.

Reaching the center of town, I stepped up onto the edge of the fountain that marked the square and looked out on the city I'd grown up in. Overwhelmed and feeling silly, I almost retreated. Taking a deep breath, I let my internal voice console me. *I can do this. I was born to do this.* Letting the reassurance wash over me, I focused on each word as I spoke.

"'There are far, far better things ahead than any we leave behind,'" I shouted. People turned to look at the crazy girl on the fountain. But soon, their concerned stares turned to recognition as they remembered things long forgotten. I looked to my sister, and her tears showed me that even she remembered what Mom had instilled in us years before. Walking back to my new family, I smiled. *Maybe Mom was right. Maybe I can be extraordinary.*

THE END

ABOUT THE AUTHOR

Faith Colleen Weaver grew up with a book in one hand and a pen in the other. Writing is in her blood and reading her ultimate escape which is why she enjoyed reading the original Choose-Your-Own-Adventure series and wished for more once she grew older. She figured, "If I can't find one, I'll write one!" Faith lives in Carlisle, PA, with her wonderful husband, John, and their three cats.

Website: faithcolleenweaver.com

Facebook: https://www.facebook.com/FaithColleenWeaver/

BIBLIOGRAPHY

Alcott, Louisa May, *Little Women*, Boston, Roberts Brothers, 1868

Austen, Jane, *Pride and Prejudice*, London, T Egerton, 1813

Barrie, J.M., *Peter and Wendy*, New York City, Charles Scribner's Sons, 1911

Bronte, Charlotte, *Jane Eyre*, London, Smith, Elder, & Co., 1847

Bronte, Emily, *Wuthering Heights*, London, Thomas Cautley Newby, 1847

Bunyan, Paul, *The Pilgrim's Progress: From this World to that Which is to Come*, London, Stationer's Register, 1678

Burnett, Frances Hodgson, *The Secret Garden*, New York, Fredrick A Stokes, 1911

Carroll, Lewis, *Alice's Adventures in Wonderland*, UK, Macmillan, 1865

Dicken, Charles, *Great Expectations*, London, Chapman & Hall, 1861

Doyle, Sir Arthur Conan, *The Adventures of Sherlock Holmes*, UK, George Newnes, 1892

Fitzgerald, F. Scott, *The Great Gatsby*, New York City, Charles Scribner's Sons, 1925

Goldman, William, *The Princess Bride*, San Diego, Harcourt Brace Jovanovich, 1973

Hawthorne, Nathaniel, *The Scarlet Letter*, Boston, Ticknor, Reed, & Fields, 1850

Hugo, Victor, *Les Miserables*, Belgium, A Lacroix, Verboeckhoven, & Cie., 1862

Kipling, Rudyard, *The Jungle Book*, UK, Macmillan, 1894

Lewis, C. S., *The Magician's Nephew*, London, The Bodley Head, 1955

London, Jack, *The Call of the Wild*, New York City, Macmillan, 1903

Mitchell, Margaret, *Gone with the Wind*, New York City, Macmillan, 1936

Montgomery, Lucy Maud, *Anne of Green Gables*, Boston, L.C. Page & Co., 1908

Orwell, George, *1984*, UK, Secker & Warburg, 1949

Saint-Exupery, Antoine, *The Little Prince*, New York City, Reynal & Hitchcock, 1943

Shakespeare, William, *A Midsummer's Nights Dream*, London, Stationer's Company, 1600

Shakespeare, William, *Romeo and Juliet*, England, 1597

Shelley, Mary, *Frankenstein*, UK, Lackington, Hughes, Harding, Mavor, & Jones, 1818

Stevenson, Robert Lewis, *Treasure Island*, London, Cassell & Company, 1883

Swift, Jonathan, *Gulliver's Travels*, London, Benjamin Motte, 1726

Tolkein, J.R.R., *The Hobbit*, Australia, George Allen & Unwin, 1937

Tolstoy, Leo, *War and Peace*, Russia, The Russian Messenger, 1869

Twain, Mark, *The Adventures of Huckleberry Finn*, London, Chatto & Windus, 1884

Tzu, Sun, *The Art of War*, China, 5th Century BC

Wilde, Oscar, *The Picture of Dorian Gray*, Philadelphia, Lippincott's Monthly Magazine, 1890

Verne, Jules, *Journey to the Center of the Earth*, France, Pierre-Jules- Hetzel, 1864